wax boats

wax boats

stories

SARAH ROBERTS

Caitlin Press

Caitlin Press Inc.
8100 Alderwood Road,
Halfmoon Bay, BC V0N 1Y1
www.caitlin-press.com

Text design by Vici Johnstone.
Cover design by Jana Curll.
Author photo Angela C. Wallace.

Printed in Canada.

Caitlin Press Inc. acknowledges financial support from the Government of Canada through the Book Publishing Industry Development Program and the Canada Council for the Arts, and from the Province of British Columbia through the British Columbia Arts Council and the Book Publisher's Tax Credit.

Library and Archives Canada Cataloguing in Publication

Roberts, Sarah, 1977-
     Wax boats / Sarah Roberts.

ISBN 978-1-894759-40-3

     I. Title.

PS8635.O227W39 2009   C813'.6   C2009-904637-7

for my family

contents

he knows where to find water	9
cougar ladies	23
tully's fish	40
hammersmith	52
drinking herman dry	75
devil hunting	87
eagle's nest	94
free is free	100
wild birds	104
the smoker	136
too long gone	158
wax boats	161
acknowledgements	173

he knows where to find water

My mother was eleven months pregnant when she decided to get me out.

"I'm going to cut this belly open myself if I have to," she threatened my father. "Do something."

My father didn't know what to do. In fact, he couldn't help but feel sheepish that it was what he had done in the first place that had put my mother in this predicament.

"The doctor promised any day now, Carol," he said, trying to squeeze between her belly and the sofa as she warmed her back at the fire.

"He said any day now two entire months ago." She would have cried except she'd tried crying in her ninth month and it hadn't helped a lick. "Garry, I am not going to carry this baby one more damn day." My mother was never a woman to swear.

There wasn't a hospital on the island. Down at the quarry there was a doctor, a morgue and a graveyard, and they could help a man who'd lost an arm under a slip of stone, but they had no advice for a woman eleven months pregnant.

The doctor my mother had seen two months previous was in the city, and although the barge that carried folks to and from the island was a modern improvement for the town, it was a less-than-reliable form of transportation. In a good chop the barge couldn't dock and folks just floated out on the rocky water until the waves wore out. In a wind the barge was easily blown off course and the trip could take hours. Some days people travelled more than others, and when the barge was full folks had to sit on the dock and wait, which could take all day.

So my father, standing at the bottom of the driveway on Granite Ridge Road, knew going to the mainland was not an option. He knew going to the quarry wouldn't help much. So he did what many men might do in a similar situation...he went to the bar.

Outside the Welcome Inn sat Clarence Dick, a man who was known to be native, but so handy with his tools and helpful with his advice he was accepted in town just the same. Only not with Bridgeworks, and Bridgeworks owned the bar.

"How's Carol?" Clarence asked as my father stepped out of his '63 Ford.

"I don't think she'll ever speak to me again."

Clarence nodded. "Don't get many eleven-month pregnancies 'round here, eh. Sure you didn't miscount?"

"I'm sure Carol knows how to count to nine, or eleven," my father said.

"So how's about a beer?" Clarence asked.

My father shook his head.

"So how's about you go in and get some beers, and then you come out and get in your truck, and you drive me up to the reserve."

"You know I can't do that, Clarence," my father said. He liked the job at the quarry.

"See, here's the thing," Clarence went on, not hearing. "You go in and get some beers, then we pick up Carol and we take her up to the reserve."

"Why would we do that?"

"Well, if the bumps in the road don't shake that kid out, maybe Auntie Mona can help."

My father had never considered Auntie Mona. He went into the bar and bought two cases.

"I guess I should have thought of that," my mother said, pulling a cardigan tight around her middle. "Well, hello, Clarence." She slid into the truck beside him. The buttons on her sweater popped off. With an open beer in one hand, Clarence picked up the lost buttons and put them in his shirt pocket as my father backed down the driveway. There were lots of bumps on the road up to the reserve but they didn't shake me loose.

My mother had to squat behind the truck a dozen times on the drive. She'd stopped wearing panties in the tenth month, to make the frequency less trouble. My mother, who almost never drank, had helped Clarence through a number of bottles by the time they could see the white church steeple and, behind it, two grey totem poles.

Auntie Mona lived in an old cedar longhouse behind the church. She had never married and she'd never had children. She lived with a household of women and all of them were called aunties, and those women had lots of children, but only girls were allowed in the house.

My mother leaned against the tailgate of the pickup, surrounded by a dozen aunties.

"This one holds on," Auntie Mona said with a smile, rubbing her fat hands around my mother's belly. My mother noticed Mona had no teeth, and one of her eyes was brown, while the other was bright green.

"Eleven months," my mother said.

"Come," said Auntie Mona.

My father followed the women as they took my mother's elbows and led her slowly into the grey rectangular building, but when he raised his foot to step through the circular doorway, Mona yelled.

"No uncles," she called from a dark place inside. My father couldn't see her or my mother, and he wanted to be reassured that she would be OK.

"No uncles," Mona called again, and my father turned away quickly, looking relieved.

Neither my mother nor my father had been on band land until that day, and my mother had certainly never been in a longhouse. When her eyes adjusted, she saw fur-lined beds covered in layers of wool blankets, woven floor mats and a large round fire at the end of the building. On the wall were newspaper photos of the Queen and Marilyn Monroe, and my mother said there was a radio playing. She was guided to the circle of stones that formed a hearth and the women at her elbows helped lower her to the dirt floor.

Mona reached for a kettle on the fire and passed my mother a cup of tea.

"This will soothe," she said.

My mother tasted alcohol and mint and there was a slight smell of roses, the tea washing through her the way water quiets flame. Mona rubbed hands over forehead and belly, singing to my mother's stomach as she drank her tea.

The aunties cooked a meal, working around Mona and my mother. A small table was placed at my mother's side and dishes were laid out. Mona coaxed my mother through every bite.

"Nettles give energy."

So my mother chewed a soggy, salty green.

"Roots for the blood," Mona whispered, and my mother bit into chalky cubes.

There was cattail, rose hips, a strange musky salad, some white fish and dried deer meat. My mother's belly had been full before she'd started eating, but she tasted a little of everything. She didn't become sick the way she had with the food she cooked at home.

Finishing her second cup of tea, my mother finally noticed how much of a fuss they were making. All the women were solemn and working, silently padding over the woven mats, carrying dishes and bowls back and forth. The house was full of children but they were extraordinarily well-behaved. They sat with their backs to the longhouse walls and did not speak.

"Are we expecting trouble?"

"No more than usual," Mona said with a grin.

It didn't take my father and Clarence long to drink the few beers they had left.

"Well, suppose we could go back to town and get some more, eh?" Clarence asked, chucking his empty bottle.

"We can't go anywhere," my father said.

"It'll be a while." Clarence jumped off the tailgate and kicked at a stray dog that ran up to him. With wide strides he walked to the entrance of Mona's longhouse, but stopped at the door and made no attempt to enter. Instead, he picked up a handful of pebbles and threw them, one at a time, at the rough cedar planks.

An auntie came to the door.

"Shoo," she said, waving her hands. "It's bad luck."

"How long?" Clarence asked, and pointed to my father.

"After midnight, we hope," the auntie replied. Then Clarence walked back to the truck.

"Got time for a run."

"I'm not leaving Carol."

"No point in staying, she's in there and the baby's in her and neither of them will leave Auntie Mona's house for a day or two, at least."

"She wouldn't want to be out here alone," my father said.

"She's not alone, Garry, she's far from that."

Leaving the reserve, they drove slowly past a group of six on the road. They were in worn jack-shirts and jeans, and they all had potato sacks thrown over their shoulders.

"Stop," said Clarence. There was no need to pull over on an empty road. Clarence got out of the truck and spoke to the group.

There were nods and smiles. Clarence came back to the truck and climbed into the cab. Behind him followed the oldest man in the group, who also climbed into the cab, while the other five flanked the sides of the pickup and jumped in the back.

"What's going on?" my father asked.

"Garry, this is Joe Dick," Clarence said. Joe Dick offered my father his hand.

"In the back there," said Clarence, "that's John Dick, Cecil Dick, Andy Dick, Daniel Dick and Larry Dick. They need a ride."

This particular group of Dicks was carried bags of fur pelts to take down to the city. They continued the family trade, selling marten for jackets the way their elders had sold beaver for top hats. A walk down-island would take all night just so they could catch the barge in the morning.

My father hoped it would be dark when they drove in to town.

"What the hell are you up to, MacDonald?" Swaney the bartender asked. My father had just ordered a couple more cases of beer. "Here you got a baby coming and you're driving around town with a truck full of Injuns?"

Swaney was a company man. If you drowned yourself at the Welcome Inn and maybe mentioned things you shouldn't, Swaney would tell Bridgeworks, that was a fact. But there was no need for my father to worry about Swaney, because Bridgeworks was there, sitting with his elbows on the granite bar.

"MacDonald, get over here," the old man ordered.

My dad left his cases on the bar and took a stool at the other end.

"How's Carol?" Bridgeworks asked.

"Bigger than your Rolls, sir," my father said. The old man chuckled.

"Saw you giving those Dicks a ride."

"Yes, sir, they're taking pelts in to the city. It's a long walk down from the reserve."

Old Man Bridgeworks waved Swaney over, who had been carefully polishing glasses.

"A beer for Garry," Bridgeworks ordered.

My father could see his truck out the window, and in the truck, Clarence Dick mouthing words along with the radio and slapping his hands against the dash.

"Looks like they forgot one," the old man said.

"No, sir, that's Clarence."

Swaney put a glass down in front of my father.

"And no baby yet?"

"Not yet, sir."

"Well, I'm taking the car into the city tomorrow. I'll pick her up and take her to the hospital. I know a good doctor."

"That's very kind of you."

"There's a good doctor in the city she can see."

"You see, sir, I don't know for sure if she'll need a doctor tomorrow, generous as your offer is."

"What do you mean?"

"Well, sir, there's some women looking after her right now, and I have a feeling, based on what they've told me, that there will be a baby by morning, sir, though I'll be sure to tell Carol how kind you've been."

Bridgeworks looked left and right, then waved Swaney away. "Old Mona, eh?"

My father nodded.

"Don't tell anyone, but I know of her. She sent some teas down to Eden when she was having St. John."

St. John was the youngest and thirteenth child in the Bridgeworks brood.

"Those Indians have their own ways of doing things," Bridgeworks continued. "Mighty handy with things like these, difficult births and such."

My father looked out the window and sipped his drink.

"Clarence Dick, sir, out in my truck, word has it he's as good a worker as anyone. Can fall a tree and knows where to fish, sir. Word has it he knows the way a cleave will crack, and where to find water in a dry field."

"Handy things to know," said Bridgeworks. "Handy things to know."

Back on the reserve, my mother had just come in from another squat behind the bushes and the aunties were lowering her down to the floor.

"Finish this," Mona said, passing a teacup. My mother didn't want to drink any more. She didn't want to eat any more. She didn't want to be sitting on the floor of a longhouse and she didn't want to be pregnant.

When the teacup was empty, Mona took it. My mother jumped as Mona slammed the cup against a plate, shaking the tea leaves loose from the side of the cup. All the aunties were standing around them, and the children were wide-eyed, holding their breath.

"See that?" Mona asked, waving a wrinkled finger to the leaves on the plate. "A pitcher means good health; happiness starts with a pitcher."

The surrounding aunties nodded. A dog barked outside.

"That's an arrow," Mona said. "And that's two upside-down hearts."

Mona wiped the loose tea off the plate and threw it into the fire.

"This child has her own mind. She will be good for the island."

"She?" my mother asked. "It's a girl?"

The aunties laughed while Mona carefully emptied her kettle onto the hot rocks surrounding the fire.

"Of course she's a girl."

My father knew Clarence was waiting for him, and beyond that, Carol was waiting too. But Bridgeworks kept buying him drinks and telling him things he didn't want to know. By now he'd learned about how Mrs. Bridgeworks, Eden, had taken an apartment in the city after St. John was born and hadn't spent a night on the island since. He'd heard about how the Bridgeworks sons fought about the family will as if the old man weren't still alive and kicking. He'd heard about how Harriet the housekeeper made the best damn porridge.

"Don't those Indians have diseases?" the old man asked abruptly.

My father glanced quickly out the window to see Clarence napping, his head against the passenger door.

"No more than the rest of us."

"Well, they'd scalp you soon as look at you, isn't that so?"

"Only certain tribes, sir, and that was back a while ago, when there was war, and only in the States."

"Well, they're good for nothing, really. Look at 'em. Every last one of them sitting around on this island like God didn't give them two hands but for scratching their own arses."

My father had been drinking for hours now.

"With all due respect, sir, I'm sure they're only idle because there's no work for them."

"Well, what do you mean; there's always work. The oceans aren't empty. The forests are still dark. Do you think I got to where I am today by drinking beer all week? No, I dug out granite. I invested in boats. I bought logging rights and set up camps. God doesn't give you anything but the opportunity."

"But sir, well, take Clarence Dick out there, sir, sleeping in my truck. He builds the best well on the island and he can always find water. He falls a dead tree so it won't land on your barn or your house. But he can't work here on Smokecrest, sir, and Smokecrest is all he knows."

"They used to carry diseases," the old man said.

"Only diseases that the settlers gave them."

"They've got those spooky grins."

"I'm sure they only want to help when they can. And the grins, well, sir, you have to admire a people who can smile when they've lost everything they had."

"It's that damn government," Bridgeworks said.

Hours later, my father stumbled out of the bar with a case of beer clinking under one arm. Old Man Bridgeworks was carrying the other case, and although Dennis, his driver, was waiting at the side of the Rolls with the door open, Bridgeworks walked to the pickup and dropped the beer in the back.

"Better let Dick drive, Garry," Bridgeworks said, rapping his knuckles against the window to wake up Clarence.

"Good evening, sir," Clarence said, suddenly sitting upright.

"Dick, you drive this man to the..." Bridgeworks stumbled. "You take this man back to his wife."

"Yes, sir," Clarence said. My father was sure that if Clarence had been wearing a hat he would have tipped it.

"And you drive safe," said Bridgeworks, moving toward the door Dennis held open for him. "This man has a baby coming. See to it he's there."

Clarence had never driven a vehicle before. My father tried to explain the intricacies of gearshifts but it was late and he'd been drinking. Finally they worked out a compromise: my father would work the gears and pedals and Clarence would hold the wheel and keep the truck on the road. They lurched forward but stalled in the pub entrance. Bridgeworks' black Rolls Royce had not moved. Finally, Dennis walked over and tapped on the truck window. My father dropped the clutch and the truck shuddered, he and Clarence splitting their sides.

"We'll give you a ride," Dennis said.

Clarence and my father each grabbed a case of beer. Dennis held the door open and my father climbed inside the car and plopped down beside Old Man Bridgeworks. Clarence stuck his head in but Dennis touched his elbow. "Best you sit up front with me, Clarence," he said.

"Oh yeah, I was just getting a peek at the back."

Dennis got into the front of the car and Clarence fumbled with his door handle.

"Take us to Carol, Dennis," Bridgeworks ordered. Dennis started the car and wound past the stalled truck in the middle of the parking lot. They drove up School Hill to the four-way stop.

"Where's Carol?" Dennis whispered to Clarence.

"The reserve."

"What the hell is she doing up there?" Dennis asked.

"For God's sake, Dennis, get a move on," Bridgeworks yelled.

Mona wanted me to be born after midnight.

"A new day is better," she said.

My mother's water broke and contractions started but the moon hadn't moved enough.

"Wait a little longer," Mona urged. The aunties sang and some of the children who were asleep against the walls opened their eyes and watched from their beds.

"I'm not waiting. I can't wait." Sweat coated my mother and she could barely speak. Mona poured water into her throat and, finally, gave her a bit of rope made of twisted bark to hold between her teeth.

Mona said I was born at two minutes after twelve.

"She's so beautiful," my mother said, holding me. She was surprised to suddenly have a baby in her arms. "I'll name her Cat."

The aunties tittered and Mona smiled.

"Cat's a good name," Mona said.

The men woke up to the rattle of pebbles being thrown at the side of the car. The bottles were empty and collected on the floor. Dennis had parked the Rolls on the St. Mary's Church lawn, just inside what used to be a little white picket fence.

My father rubbed his eyes and sat up. Clarence opened the car door.

"The baby came," said one of the kids who'd been throwing pebbles.

"Everything alright?" Clarence asked, putting his hands on the tops of two heads and leaning on them like crutches.

"Auntie Mona's been singing all morning."

"Good, good. Well, who's got coffee on?"

The children jumped up and down, each of them offering their mother's kitchen to receive the guests.

"Follow me," Clarence said, sticking his head in the car. "Coffee's on, we'll get breakfast."

Bridgeworks stepped out slowly and kept one hand on the cold roof as he surveyed his situation. "Guess we'd better fix that, Dennis," he said, looking at the bits of broken fence under his whitewall tires.

My father followed Clarence along the trail, past leaning houses and rusting vehicles. Dennis walked behind my father, and behind Dennis, Old Man Bridgeworks. Behind Bridgeworks was a line of children that went all the way down the reserve. Some had stayed to watch the car and witness Father Crane's reaction to the broken fence. But most of them walked behind Bridgeworks, brown eyes wide, silent, and smiling.

"That's a good breakfast, ma'am," Bridgeworks said. He wiped his mouth with his sleeve and dropped his fork to the table. It had been a long time since he'd eaten off a tin plate, a long time since he'd drunk all night and slept in his clothes. Clarence had taken them back to his house, where his wife Hannah had coffee waiting, eggs in the pan, and warm bannock on the table when they came in the door.

She chose not to speak that morning, although my father knew from what Clarence had told him that she could say a lot when she wanted to speak.

"When can I see Carol and the baby?" my father asked.

Clarence shrugged. "There's no knowing. Mona will send them out when they're ready."

Dennis had never eaten a meal with Bridgeworks before, and while he normally might have chatted warmly with Clarence and my father, that morning his head hurt and he didn't want to offend his boss. Hannah cleared the table and the men went outside for a smoke. My father didn't smoke regularly but he tried it then, sitting on the porch of Clarence's house, looking out at the water and the shoulders of the island.

"That's a good beach you have there, Clarence," Bridgeworks said.

"Yes, sir, we catch some big fish out there." No one had bothered with "sir" in the car.

"I've heard you're real handy when it comes to wells."

"I've dug a few 'round here."

Bridgeworks belched. "I could use a man who was handy."

Dennis and my father looked at each other.

"Can you handle horses?"

"I've been around 'em, sir."

"I guess you should come by the house tomorrow then," Bridgeworks said. "Come by and see Dennis, we'll put you on salary."

Dennis nodded and Clarence nodded and my father watched the sea.

"We should go have a talk with that priest, Dennis," Bridgeworks said, standing. "Someone will have to pay for a new fence, I suspect."

The four men walked back to the car. It was surrounded, not by children this time, but by Mona and my aunties. My mother stood with me in her arms, her cardigan tightly closed with new bone buttons.

cougar ladies

All fall Agnes felt shadowed by the traplines. The thought of following them every few days, all winter long, made her tired. She didn't want to do it any more but she couldn't tell Mabel. She'd spent the season saying nothing. Mabel never noticed.

They took care of the cabin and animals. Mabel did her baking. Agnes worked the garden. At night they'd tell stories about the homesteader who'd brought camels to the island. Sometimes they'd make shadow puppets against the cabin walls before blowing out the lamp and curling into their cots.

It was a night such as that, with Mabel on one side of the room and Agnes on the other, the door propped open for a bit of a breeze, and their dog Chaucer asleep on the step, that Agnes tried to explain.

"We're not spring chickens any more," Agnes said suddenly.

"What are you babbling about?" Mabel asked.

"The traplines."

"What about them?"

"Well, what do we do them for, anyway?"

Mabel snorted. "We do them because we always do them."

"I just thought—" Agnes stopped.

"What do you think?"

"I just don't know if we should bother."

"We do them every year," Mabel said. "What would we have to trade without them? How would we get our sugar and flour, or our lamp oil for that matter?"

"We could get those things."

"I don't know what father raised you, Agnes Vincent, but mine taught me not to rely on charity."

The sisters lay silent. Then Agnes spoke softy. "Mabel, we might die soon."

"That may be true," Mabel said quickly, "but I ain't dead yet."

After that, Mabel became the silent sister. They agreed to scale down from two traplines to one. Agnes made preparations for another winter with a lightness in her heart and never noticed Mabel's mood.

"You've never been down by yourself," Agnes said. "Do we need flour?"

Mabel shook her head. She'd been busying herself with a round cut of tarp, punching holes along the top and weaving a rope through.

"Do you need to go to the doctor?"

"Nope," Mabel said. Pulling the rope tight, she made a purse out of the tarp. She walked to the side of the barn and hung the purse from a rusty nail on the end of a beam.

"The dentist?" Agnes asked. Mabel shook her head. She picked up a bucket and walked to the well. Mabel dropped a pumpkin-sized boulder down the shaft. There was a splinter song as ice cracked and gave way. She pulled up the wet rope and poured water into her bucket. She carried the bucket to the tarp purse.

"Then why are you going down?" asked Agnes. Mabel continued to pull water up from the well and transfer it to her tarp. "Why do you want to go down without me?"

Despite ankle-deep snow covering the field, Mabel undressed and stood naked under the tarp. "It's none of your business," she said. Then she stabbed the bottom of the tarp with a knife and hooted as ice cold water rained down.

Each spring they went down with furs. They sold marten and beaver, occasionally a bearskin. And even long after it was illegal to do so, the sisters brought down one cougar skin a year.

Until the mid-thirties, folks could bring pelts to the Bridge-works Dry Goods and General Store. Trapping declined on the island after the Second World War as everyone took up jobs on the water, in the logging camps, or tunnelling into stone.

But Bridgeworks never stopped trading with the twins. When the sisters made their spring pilgrimage down the moun-tain, whatever they carried with them was bought. Whatever they needed was sold at cost.

To town folk, who knew about this arrangement, it made perfect sense that the miser would be generous to the two people who were furthest removed from island society. No one but Bridgeworks liked the sisters. They spat on the sidewalk and lacked refined manners. Not only did they look dirty, but they smelled too. When they went hunting they brushed their skin with willow bark. But Agnes and Mabel never put much impor-tance on washing up when they knew they'd just be elbow-deep in it the next day.

Their down-island visits were short. They posed with their rifles and golden cougar pelt for the annual newspaper photo. Then they walked back up the mountain. When the forest trail opened to their field and barn they relaxed the way most island-ers do when the ferry pulls away from the city docks.

"When are you coming back?" Agnes asked as Mabel emptied the money tin into her satchel.

"Couldn't say," said Mabel.

"So what, I'm to check the lines and run the farm while you go off on some mad adventure?"

"I'm just going down-island, Agnes. You're as good a shot as I am. I suspect if tonight while I'm in town there is a sudden invasion of our hillside, you'll be able to protect the farm."

"Don't do anything stupid," spat Agnes.

"I suppose I could say the same to you," said Mabel, then took up her satchel and walked out the door.

The Welcome Inn was across the road from the general store. Pub windows looked out over the water and offered a view of the island's hunched shoulders.

Mabel remembered when the RCMP station was a one-room shack across from the Inn, beside the general store. It was a location of convenience. Loggers used to come down from the camps and pass out drunk at the Inn. The jail across the road meant less distance for the officers to drag them. But as the island expanded, so did the RCMP's scope. A larger detachment had been built up School Hill in the sixties.

Mabel had never been in the bar before. At the heavy wooden doors at the top of the dock, a young man sat on a stool.

"Hold it," he said as Mabel reached for the door. "You can't bring *that* in here."

Mabel looked down at Chaucer, panting at her side. "Stay boy," she ordered. Chaucer sat.

"No, I mean *that*," he said. He pointed to the rifle Mabel held across her left shoulder.

"What am I supposed to do with it then?" Mabel could see a sign on the door behind the man that said: No Guns, No Knives,

No Fighting.

"I guess you could leave it with me. I'll put it behind the bar and you can have it when you go."

"Fine," she said, emptying ammunition into her hand.

"What do you have it for, anyway?"

"Bears."

"No bears inside," he said. Then he pointed to the leather case Mabel wore on her belt. "No knives allowed, either."

"Fine, here." She passed it over.

"Have a nice night," he said, and pulled the door open.

"Hold on," said Mabel. She bent, lifted up the leg of her suede pants. She unsnapped her ankle holster and handed over another knife. "I guess you'd better take this one, too."

He looked impressed. "Anything in your bag?"

"Just bullets. They won't do much damage, even if I throw them."

The Inn was one long room, with a row of windows that faced the dock and a long granite bar running its length. A band crowded into one corner and pounded out music.

Mabel sat at the first empty barstool. The bartender hid his belly in a garish tropical-print shirt. He wiped the counter.

"What can I get you?"

"A beer."

"What kind?"

"There are different kinds of beer?"

The bartender grinned and hooked a thumb through a loop in his jeans. "We've got Bud, Blue, Canadian, Coors Lite, Kokanee Gold, Kilkenny, Shaftsbury, Guinness, Rickard's Red, Sleeman's Honey Brown, and Okanagan Pale Ale on tap."

"An ale," said Mabel.

Up the mountain, Agnes thought she heard raccoons in the compost.

"Damn that sister," she said, putting down her book and cup of tea. "If she hadn't gone gallivanting..."

She pulled on her galoshes and turned up the lantern. "Well, if that darn dog was here, there wouldn't be any need..." She went out toward the barn. The scraps pile was untouched. The only tracks in the snow were her own.

The bartender plunked a glass in front of Mabel.

"On the house," he said, then walked back down to the middle of the bar and stood with his hands on his hips like a soldier at ease.

A circle of girls wearing shoes close to stilts danced in front of the band. Most of the tables were full of men in dirty boots and flannel shirts rubbed thin at the elbows. Surveying the room, Mabel was sure she was the oldest one there. But then another old-timer stood up from his seat at the far end of the bar.

"Cigarette?" he asked, holding up a pack. She took one and put it in her mouth. The man lit a match.

"Don't smoke, do ya?" he asked. He had a long beard that was white at his face and black at the tips, streaked yellow and brown in between.

"Those are some interesting duds you got on," he pointed to Mabel's pants and her moccasins with tasselled toes.

"Made 'em myself," said Mabel.

"They'd look good on my floor," he said, smiling.

Mabel thought about this for a moment. "Get lost," she announced.

He laughed. "Let me buy ya a beer."

"I've got my own money," said Mabel. "Skedaddle."

When she had finished her first glass the bartender brought

another without her asking. He wouldn't take her money.

"Those things aren't even in circulation no more," he said as she pressed her one and two dollar bills toward him.

"My money's no good?"

"On the house, like I said."

Both sisters had used indoor plumbing. It wasn't all that different from their outhouse, which had a door and a seat. They used paper from books both of them had read and weren't likely to read again. The principle was the same. Once, when Mabel had been younger, she'd used the indoor bathroom at the government agent's office. There were two doors, side by side, and each had a figure on the front. The figure on the right wore a triangular dress, and the one on the left stood stiffly in pants. Mabel understood the concept. She was wearing pants. She chose the door on the left. Since then Mabel had always been sure to squat on the trail before she got to town.

But after her first beer she knew she'd never be able to hold it until she reached the bush again. She walked cautiously around tables and found the bathroom empty. When she looked at the wall she was startled to see Agnes somehow standing there, glaring at her.

"What are you doing here?" Mabel asked herself. "Oh, it's just a mirror."

Then she stared, shocked at the wild woman looking back. A few extra pounds meant a warmer winter and a little grit showed hard work. But she didn't like *looking* old.

"What's the use?" she asked, washing her hands under warm water and drying them against the seat of her pants. She moved back into the bar room and sipped at another glass.

The only person who looked as miserable as Mabel was a young girl in a corner surrounded by three denim-dressed men.

She wore a pink dress and black heeled shoes. She had an unbuttoned jean jacket and her hair was pulled back in a high ponytail. Mabel could see her nails reflect pink.

The men around her were loud, emptying their glasses quickly. As they cheered and pounded the table, the girl watched the dancers who, Mabel thought, flailed around like a catch of fish that hadn't been hit on the head yet.

A man sitting across from the girl saw her watching the dance floor. He spoke and she shook her head. He stood in the aisle and put a hand on her upper arm. She pulled her arm free and the other men at the table laughed. Red flushed into the standing man's face. He grabbed her shoulder again, pulling her up from her seat and out in front of the band.

That was when the singer announced it was the last song. Finishing her glass, Mabel moved toward the young man who'd stopped her when she'd come in. He was sitting on the inside of the Inn's wooden doors.

"I need my knives and my gun back."

"I don't think I should give them to you."

"What kind of racket are you running here? I'm leaving and I want them back."

"Maybe you're too drunk. Maybe if I give them back I'll be charged for being irresponsible."

"It's irresponsible to say you'll give something back and not do it. That's theft. Want me to call the cops?"

Mabel had never used a phone before. She wished it were forty years earlier, when she could lean her head out the door and just yell.

"No need, no need," he said, holding up a hand. "How about you go home and sleep it off, come back tomorrow and I'll give you your gun and knives?"

"Going home involves a five-hour walk up the mountain to

the north side. A walk I certainly ain't doing without my gun or my knives. This is highway robbery. I want my gun and my knives back now."

"How do I know I can trust you?"

"You damn well trusted me to hand them over in the first place. So I suspect you can trust that once I get my gear back, I'll leave and you won't ever have to look at my old face again."

He stood, walked to a back room, and returned. The band had stopped playing and the bar was mostly empty. The room lights were on and the waitress cleared tables.

"Have a safe night," he said, as he handed back Mabel's things. She reloaded her rifle, fixed her knife back onto her belt and fitted her ankle holster into place.

"Good riddance," Mabel said, pushing open the door. Chaucer came quickly to her side. Then he looked toward the parking lot and growled.

"I'm not going!" a high voice yelled.

"Shut up and get in the truck," a man shouted back.

"You're drunk and I'm not going anywhere with you. Fuck off."

Mabel heard a slap and a stifled cry. Cautiously, with her rifle out in front of her and a growling dog at her side, Mabel walked into the dark parking lot.

"You stupid bitch, you're more trouble than you're worth."

"Just leave me alone, Darryl, you're drunk. I'm tired of this."

Mabel got close enough to see them. It was the pretty girl in the pink dress standing next to a shiny new pickup. The passenger door was open and the cab light shone over them.

"Well, I'm goddamn sick of you whining all the time. What the hell do you want from me?"

"Nothing," she yelled. "I want you to leave me alone. I don't want to see you any more. I don't want you to talk to me, or my friends. I want to pretend you and me never happened."

She spoke with loathing. "You know what you did? You lowered my stock. Before I was a nice girl with nice friends. I had a good reputation, and ever since we started dating, people have been shaking their heads. I finally understand why."

He raised his hand and flung it across her face. Mabel took a step forward, but then stopped. She'd stalked animals all her life, but she'd never watched people.

"Go ahead and hit me," the girl said. "It's the last chance you'll get."

He hit her with one hand and then the other, grabbed a shoulder and pulled her into his fist. She fell and he kicked her against the truck tire.

"Hit her again and I'll splatter you across the parking lot," Mabel said, stepping closer.

"Fuck off," he yelled, but then he spun around, saw the gun and immediately threw up his arms. "Whoa, lady, this ain't none of your business. This is between my girl and me. So why don't you just wander back to the retirement home and put that thing over the fireplace?"

"You okay?" Mabel asked the girl, who slowly pulled herself up.

"Fine," she said, moving away from the truck and taking cover behind Mabel. "Just shoot him," she said as she wiped blood from her nose.

"Fuck, Lanna," he squeaked. "This is no time for joking."

But Mabel could tell Lanna wasn't joking at all, so without much thought, she squeezed the trigger.

"Holy fuck, lady, you could have killed me." Darryl was face-down on the concrete. The front window of the truck cab had shattered and sprayed glass all over. Lanna was laughing. The massive bartender, and a few others, came running toward them. Chaucer wouldn't stop barking.

Mabel couldn't believe it.

"Good one, lady," Lanna giggled. "That'll teach him."

Darryl yelled for someone to call the cops.

"Let's get out of here," Lanna said to Mabel.

Mabel slung her rifle over her shoulder but not before eyeing it with suspicion. She'd been shooting since she was eight years old. They started walking up the hill, away from the Inn.

"I'm Lanna."

"Mabel."

"You a Cougar Lady?"

Mabel nodded. "I guess so."

"So what were you doing down at the bar?"

"Looking for a man," she said with a shrug.

Lanna laughed. "What would you want one of them for?"

"Never had one."

"So why did you have a gun at the bar?"

"I don't go without it."

"Well I'm glad you had it tonight. He can get pretty out of control sometimes. And when he's drunk there's nothing stopping him. If you hadn't fired that warning shot, there's no telling what shape I'd be in."

"It wasn't a warning shot," said Mabel. "I've never missed before."

"You meant to shoot him?"

"You told me to."

"But I was joking."

"Didn't sound like it."

A car came down the hill, flashing red and blue lights.

"You better not tell anyone," said Lanna. "Tell them it was a warning shot."

The car stopped in the road with headlights on the pair. Two cops got out with their firearms drawn.

"It's not loaded," called Mabel.

"Drop it and freeze," they yelled.

They scolded her for shooting below the power lines and for not having a birth certificate or driver's licence.

"We'll have to make some calls," said the man in uniform as he guided Mabel into a cell. "Sleep it off."

Mabel had never spent a night off the mountain. There was no sleep. She sat on the cold bench and stared at the closed door beyond her cell bars for hours until it finally opened. A short man with white hair walked his cane over to the cell. He looked familiar.

"What are you up to, lady?" he asked. Then he tilted his head to one side. "You Agnes or Mabel?"

"Who's asking?"

"You don't know me?"

Mabel thought she did but didn't like to say when she wasn't sure.

"I promised that daft father of yours all those years ago to let you alone up on that mountain, and you don't know me to look at me, then?"

"Bridgeworks?"

"Aye, lass," he said softly.

"I thought for sure you'd be dead by now."

"Close enough, they keep telling me."

Mabel stood and stretched her arms up to the cell ceiling. "How'd you know where I was?"

"I know everything around here," he said. Mabel snorted.

"But I hadn't heard about your sister. I'm sorry."

"What about her?"

"Surely she's gone?"

Mabel snorted again. "I come down by myself and you all think she's dead."

"You mean she's not?"

"No, I just wanted to come down alone."

"What for?"

"An adventure."

Bridgeworks waved toward the cell and wiggled one grey eyebrow.

"Let's get us a coffee," Bridgeworks suggested as they left the station. A driver held open the door of a black car. Bridgeworks handed the driver his cane and lowered himself down to the leather seat.

"I'll walk."

"Get in."

"No, I should be getting up the mountain."

"I want to talk to you, now get in."

Bridgeworks sat with the car door open and Mabel stood on the sidewalk.

"So why did you come down, then?" he asked.

Mabel had all kinds of answers, but the one that leapt past her lips was not the one she'd intended.

"We're going to die soon."

"True enough," he said. "Soon enough."

Bridgeworks told her about an arrangement he could make in town. "I've been thinking of you a lot over the past years, since they gave me this damn cane. It's not an easy life you gals have made for yourselves. There's a few private places down here with electricity and running toilets."

"We've done just fine and we'll keep on that way."

"Talk it over with Agnes," Bridgeworks said.

"I better get on home," said Mabel.

"Come down again soon, before the snow melts."

Mabel slapped the side of her leg to signal her dog. Looking up the mountain, she saw grey cover that weighed down the sky. "Looks like snow," she said to the sidewalk and started up the hill.

Snow had fallen another foot overnight. Agnes woke to a muted mountain. She stoked the wood stove and made twice the porridge and tea she needed. The twins had checked the lines two mornings ago, and Agnes knew she'd have to go out. They didn't like leaving an animal caught or injured for long. That just made it bait for some larger, meaner hunter.

"I'm too old for this," Agnes mumbled, putting on her fur coat and rubber galoshes. But then, looking out the window at the limbs of cedar trees bent low with snow, Agnes undressed again. She expected Mabel would be home before noon, which gave them a few hours before dark to check the lines.

The field was flat and white, looking oddly warm under such a low cover of cloud. Agnes remembered the massive stumps her father had burned from the ground. It took years to carve one flat, open patch of land from the misty rainforest. Down in town most people thought the island was named after stump fires from the Vincent farm, which billowed black from the crest.

By one-thirty, Agnes realized Mabel might not come back at all. "Could have at least left the dog," she said, pulling her warmer layers back on. She crossed the field in snowshoes and entered a tight trail that closed in on itself with growth every spring.

Agnes supposed it was at the general store where she'd heard about old age pensions and retirement homes. At the time she'd said to herself that she'd rather die on the mountain than end up in a place for geezers. And she hadn't changed her mind much on that score, except some mornings. When her fingers throbbed and curled into themselves she thought maybe store-bought bread wouldn't be so bad. And maybe, on cold mornings, it would be nice not to have to bring in wood for the stove.

She turned off the main trail and began pushing through a deer-trail of salal and fern. She'd loop around the line and check for tracks.

"Here I am minutes younger," Agnes said to the snow, "and who's out on the trail and taking care of things? And who's down in the town like some tarty schoolgirl?" What hurt Agnes most was not Mabel's sudden need to be alone, but the suggestion that her motives were none of Agnes's business. Agnes suddenly felt as if she'd lived her life too bare. All these years, she'd shared every thought with Mabel, expecting that Mabel was doing the same.

"And all this time maybe she was keeping secrets," Agnes muttered. She sat on the top of an icy stump and sucked on her water jug. She had a slice of smoked ham in her pocket. She took it out and chewed off a chunk.

She hadn't come across any tracks. She'd been out for over two hours and would soon be finished her loop, coming out on the main trail close to where she'd left it. Usually in winter there was mountain music as clumps of snow dropped from cedar boughs and the occasional Steller's jay squawked. Agnes was aware of the absence of sound beyond her breath and plodding snowshoes.

As the day slipped into darkness, she pushed through a grove of bare huckleberry bush back to the narrow main trail. Up ahead, toward the farm, she could see the marks she'd made stretching through the snow. Agnes moved on, but when she crossed her own tracks, she saw a second set that were not hers. Some shadow creature followed at the beginning of the loop. Agnes spun around and squinted through the greying evening. Five marks in the snow came out from the other end of the loop and then ended abruptly. Agnes pulled her gun from her shoulder and looked up into the trees around her.

"You bored or just crazy?" Agnes called out, walking backward down the trail. "You're a long way out of the forest. Just playing, or are you really that hungry?"

It was slower walking the trail backward with her gun pointed into the forest.

"What's this about, following me all afternoon?" Agnes remembered when she'd stopped, leaned against a stump and gnawed at her ham. "You've got to be pretty old if that wasn't the perfect time to pounce," she said to the trees, then shuddered.

Just when Agnes was thinking how silly she must look, stomping backward through the snow, she heard a familiar sound. Agnes whistled, and Chaucer came running up the trail.

The dog wagged his tail and sniffed Agnes. Then, sensing something on the wind, Chaucer stiffened. He bared his teeth at the trail Agnes had just covered and growled.

"Still there, eh?" Agnes mumbled. She could hear Mabel up the trail, closer to home, whistling for the dog. Chaucer used his hind legs to pull himself through the snow, never blinking while he threatened the blackness behind them.

Mabel came into view, her lantern glowing against the snow and cedars.

"There's a cougar behind me," said Agnes.

"How far?"

"Darn close. Been on my tail since I started the loop."

Mabel passed Agnes and the growling dog.

"Don't bother," Agnes said.

"I'm checking the tracks."

"I can tell you right now not to bother. Let's get home."

They walked quickly to where dense rainforest broke open into field.

"How could you let it follow you the whole loop?"

"You're the one who took the dog."

"What were the tracks like?"

"Long, light. An old one."

"Can't catch mice any more." They stepped over their old tracks toward the cabin.

"I'd like to think we're harder to hunt than mice," said Agnes. "Maybe it was playing."

"Yes, cats do get curious," Mabel said softly. The instinct to hunt snapped her mind like a snare. She wouldn't mention Bridgeworks' offer. "Good thing that cat's old," she said. "We'll catch it later, next time we're out."

tully's fish

"*We're not* going up there, are we?"

Dad had the fishing gear under one arm. We stood at the base of the wooden dam, spattered by small waterfalls pouring from cracks in the old beams.

"Just climb the spikes," Dad said. He adjusted the fishing gear and began pulling himself up with one arm.

The wood was moss-covered and punky. "I can't."

"Sure you can, Thomas. Look, the trout are caught above this dam. There's granite on all sides. We go up the face."

It was true that the riverbed was a field of massive granite boulders, like God's collection of oversized golf balls, slate grey and water smoothed. No one could climb them.

As he one-armed himself to the top, Dad called down to me. "Come on."

I was soaking wet. "I'm scared."

He pretended not to hear me. He stood on the top of the dam, looked down, and called again. His voice seemed to echo over the rock and water, caught in the evergreens. We were after cutthroat trout. Every spring Dad caught one from the top of Smoke Creek, above the waterfall and past the dam. This was the first year I'd been invited along and I'd been given a new featherweight rod for the occasion. We had a jar of salmon roe bought off a fish boat at the government wharf; until that morning he'd never told me what he used for bait.

I twisted one hand against the first spike and pulled away a fistful of flaked iron rust that scraped red into my skin.

"Just climb straight up," he bellowed from above.

I tucked my new rod into my armpit just like he had and pulled myself up from the granite base. As soon as my feet left the stone, the sounds of the creek and the forest became much louder. The water seemed to rush faster, the wind in the cedars seemed colder, the light mist in the air stung my face. My rubber-soled sneakers slipped against the spikes and rotten wood, but I made progress, and worked my way to the top, white knuckled.

"That's it, boy. You made it!" He reached down and caught the back of my jacket, tugging me up over the lip of the dam. I was out of breath and unsure of how we'd get down. I sat with my feet dangling over the edge.

"Who built this?"

"Miners. Back in grandpa's day."

"A big dam like this?" I thought miners used little sluice boxes.

"Maybe loggers. I don't know. But this is where the fishing's good. Generations of cutthroat caught up here, away from everything. Come on." He balanced along the thin wooden lip of the dam. "We'll go up this side."

We pushed through alder, salmonberry, thistle, ferns. The boulders in the river looked more inviting than pushing through a new trail, but they were moss and dew covered, slick and hard, impossible to climb. We stomped through the mud.

"Bear," Dad warned, kicking the toe of his boot into a pile on the ground. It was black but speckled with undigested seeds from red berries. "Watch out." He continued through the bush without another word, following the river until he finally turned toward it.

We reached a flat shelf of granite that hunched over a swirling green pool. "This is the place," Dad said eagerly. "Look at that, an entire family of untouched fish raised on clear mountain water. These ones like to fight." He pulled the jam jar of red roe from his pocket, shook out a handful of eggs, and tossed them into the water.

"To get them started." The fish swarmed. "So, fit three or four eggs onto the hook." I followed his directions and squished the slimy orbs onto the barbed tip. "Just toss it in. That's it. The right spot, the right bait, a man doesn't need anything else."

I tossed the tip of the rod over the pool and let the line loose. Dad took a small net from the pocket inside his jacket and shook it out.

"What makes the water so green?"

"Moss. All the moss on the boulders filters the water and makes it that clear green."

As he finished speaking, a raw cackle, like an undone laugh, burst from the lush cover on the far side of the pool. I stiffened.

"Who's there?" Dad called across the creek. "Did you hear that?" he asked me. I nodded and pointed across the twenty-foot chasm of water. Something had moved between the boulders.

"Dad." This time I saw a shadow first, then a slow lumbering shape moving between the lichen-covered boulders. "What is it?"

Dad shrugged and stared across the creek. His hand absently went to his belt, where he flicked open the leather case and removed his knife. The shape on the other side of the water split in two. A tall thin man dressed in clothes that looked ragged, hand-made, leaned his belly against the arc of a grey boulder and did not move. He watched us as if we couldn't see him.

The other shape had the form of a bear, but it wasn't a grizzly—no hump. And it wasn't a black bear either, not chocolate colour with a coal nose.

"Is it a polar bear?" I whispered, not wanting the man on the other side of the water to hear.

Dad shushed me. The bear had a pink nose and pink pads on its broad paws. Its fur was snowy white, broken only by a thick black strip around its neck that looked like a collar. The bear glared across the water at us and lifted its nose to catch a scent. A man would have a difficult time crossing the creek, with the cold, swirling water and the smooth, slippery boulders. But a bear was meant for those conditions. If it wanted to cross, it would cross.

Just as I opened my mouth to ask Dad what he was planning to do, the tip of my rod bent, the handle pulled in my hand, and the line spun out with a thrilling "zee" sound. I tugged the pole to my chest and braced the reel. The bear's ears cocked towards the noise and sudden action. My instinct was to bring the fish in, but as soon as I began winding, I doubted myself.

"What do I do?"

Dad looked at the bear and then glanced downstream. Between him and the truck, with its locked doors and rifle rack, was an obstacle course of rushing water, slime-covered rocks the size of houses, thorny bush and a rotting dam.

"Well, bring it in," he said, never looking away from the bear. The cackling laugh exploded from the man on the other side, trying to chameleon himself against stone.

I fought the cutthroat. It flashed its fins, pulled me toward the ledge and surged on the line when I pulled it back. It swished white water with its tail and the bear moved to the water's edge and stretched out one languid front paw. I thought I could smell the musty odour of its fur, coated in mist and drying in shafts of sun.

The man cackled again, and it bothered me that Dad hadn't said a word about it. "Did you hear that?" I asked.

But Dad was busy leaning over the stone ledge, one arm stretched out into the middle of the pool, his small net dwarfed by the size of the powerful fish.

"Pull it in, keep on it."

Only a fraction of the fish would fit in the net.

"Dad, what about that guy?"

Another laugh shimmied from rock to rock, loose and unbuckled. The bear dipped a wide paw into the creek and flexed its claws in the direction of the fish.

Belly-down against stone, Dad reached with the net. "Almost got it," he groaned. "Bring it in a little more." I pulled against the line with the weight of my entire body and he managed to scoop the head of the fish. With a swift, arcing swing of his arm, he lifted the catch from the water and dropped it onto the rock, tangled in nylon net.

At the same time the bear hefted itself up, first onto all fours and then only to its hind legs, pawing the air. Dad was about to bring a small rock down onto the head of the flapping fish when the bear roared. It held its legs still in the air while the rough growl filled the bank of the creek and seemed to shake the tops of the trees.

As the roar subsided, the man on the other side of the creek pulled himself away from behind his boulder, and moved toward the bear. He was hairy, caked in mud. His clothes were ragged and patched together. He wore a shapeless oil-skin hat and boots with moccasin soles that laced up the front of his legs.

I had not yet let go of my rod handle as the man bounced across the rocks on his side of the stream. As if it were perfectly normal, something that everyone did all the time, the man came up to the side of the white bear, grabbed hold of the leather strap around its neck, and pulled himself over the massive, furry shoulders, so that he sat astride.

It didn't take a second. Just one leap from the bear into the water and one leap out. Perhaps if the pool had been a bit smaller, the bear could have cleared it in one jump. Dad and I both stepped to the back of the granite shelf, so our shoulders pushed against the bushes. "If we have to run," Dad whispered, as the bear heaved itself and rider up onto the ledge, "make sure to split up."

The man rolled himself off the bear, and picked up the fish in the net, still attached by line to the rod in my hands. "Tully's fish," he said loudly. Then he bit the line off with his teeth and climbed back onto the bear, swinging the net over his shoulder. The bear moved forward and Dad and I backed away, trying to put space between ourselves and the approaching pair.

The thick scent of wet fur and mud and fish and forest pushed past. Massive haunches brushed against my shoulder as the bear and rider broke into the greenery and left us standing on the granite ledge.

Neither of us moved. A flicker swooped down along the water's edge. It was hearing the cackling laugh again, this time from a distance, that brought us back.

"Do we run?" I asked.

Dad shook his head. He took my rod from my hands, reeled in the loose line, and placed it on the ground. "You know those mountain men you hear about?" Dad asked quietly. "Well that was one of them. I've never seen anything like it."

The man was believable. The bear wasn't.

"Let's go home," I said.

Dad shook his head again. "Don't you want to see how he lives?"

I told him I didn't.

"Come on, Thomas," Dad said. He left our gear on the ledge

and stepped into the forest. "No one's going to believe us, so we might as well see for ourselves."

I didn't understand his point but knew I had to follow. The bear tracks were easy to trace; they led around the goliath trunks of cedar trees, over fern and moss-covered ground, then up a hill, and around the base of a steep stone bluff. The air was still moist from the creek, and the hush of moving water still echoed around the trees. But at the top of the bluff the air changed to dry, pine-needle wind. We moved under the embrace of a high canopy, and came into a clearing, worn bare like a much-used backyard. A small hut leaned against a natural stone wall on the far side of the clearing, with smoke tufting from the roof.

Dad pulled me down to hide behind a mound of thick bracken. I could smell his sweat through his flannel shirt. His breathing slowed as he studied the clearing. Everything was in shadow, under the broad cover of trees grown tight at their tops. Beneath this dense canopy was a dark, open meadow. A fat peacock and four peahens stood beside the hut, bowing their heads to the forest floor. The long streak of a ferret's tail slashed across the ground as it rolled under a tree stump. A donkey with a knotted coat full of twigs stood on the far side of the clearing. A yearling buck, still wearing its white baby spots, slept with its velvet muzzle curled into its side.

The flap on the hut was pulled aside and the man leaned his head out in our direction. "No point in hiding," he said, then choked out a loud cackling laugh. "Tully's got tea."

Dad slowly rose from behind the ferns and I followed him.

"Don't drink anything," he whispered as he moved toward the hut. "Where's the bear?" Dad asked the man.

"Ghost bear's gone." The man opened his arms as if he were about to offer a hug. "Out to play."

Dad stopped walking.

"Tully's got tea," the man said again, this time waving us into his hut.

Dad shook his head and turned to me. "We best be going."

"Tea, I made tea."

Just then a screech filled the air. We looked up and the man stuck out his arm. A sparrow hawk, a tiny, knife-beaked bird, landed on the man's outstretched arm and studied us with cold eyes.

"How'd you do that?" Dad asked. He'd always been fascinated by hawks. He turned back to face the man. "You train it?" Dad waved a hand to the menagerie in the clearing. "You train all these?"

The man shook his head and stroked the neck of the small bird. "Tully makes friends. Come in for tea."

"We're leaving," Dad said, gruff again. "Enjoy the fish."

We stopped back at the fishing spot to collect our gear. There were endless questions I had about the man and the bear, but neither of us spoke the entire trip home.

"Dad, I want to go back."

We were in the workshop with the radio mumbling between us. I was trying to splice rope as he sharpened the teeth on his long saw.

"We've got work to do."

"Don't you want to know where I want to go?"

"No."

"I want to go see that Tully guy. You know, up the river."

"Let me tell you something, Thomas. A man doesn't live up the mountain like that for no reason."

"I think he wanted friends."

"Doesn't matter."

I watched him work.

"I thought you said it was wrong to be afraid of the strange, just because it's strange. Isn't that what you're doing?"

Dad removed his glasses and wiped his palm over his forehead and back against the leather of his skull.

"Thomas, things aren't always what they seem, and I think, in a situation like this, it's best to walk away before anything bad happens. I know another fishing hole. Forget the weirdo." It was Dad who'd wanted to follow the man and I didn't understand what had changed his interest. Dad was always seeing things I didn't.

Of course there was no forgetting. Every day I saw something that reminded me of the mountain man: a hippie in a dirty leather tunic at Harvey's gas station; a sparrow hawk swooping across the road at dusk. I snuck out at night and removed the bait from Dad's raccoon traps, hoping to save them.

The summer burned away into fall windstorms and it was one of those rainy, windy mornings when I heard the coyote howling. There is no mistaking a coyote—that wild, solemn cry. Dad was on the water and Mom was out. I put on my rain slicker and went searching.

A coyote is a tiny, scrawny, wild dog with a reputation for being clever. This one was only a pup though, huddled at the base of our oak tree, licking its back right leg and then crying out from the pain. The leg was a bloody stump, either shot off, bitten off, or ripped off in a trap. The coyote pup bared its teeth at me and tried to limp away when I first got close. But after one step it collapsed against the tree trunk and shattered the hushing rain with another cry.

Dad would have shot it. He'd say there was no place for an injured animal in the world except to die a slow, sad death. Then he'd say coyotes aren't worth saving, with the trouble they cause to chicken coops and house cats. He'd tell me he was doing the coyote a favour and then he'd get his gun.

But Dad wasn't there.

The neighbours grew a patch of plants in their greenhouse that they called tomatoes but were clearly something else. I'd heard stories of injured deer and rabbits eating those plants to dull pain, so I snuck into the greenhouse, slid a mesh shelf out of the plywood drying box, and filled a pocket with the sticky green buds.

I searched our house for the hammock-style harness my mother called a snuggle. It was a kind of backwards papoose that wrapped around the shoulder and held a baby tight to the chest. Mom carried my little sister that way, before she got too big for it. In our kitchen, I rolled pieces of chicken around the sticky buds.

The coyote ate the pieces so fast if probably didn't notice the stuffing. I waited half an hour, sitting in the rain. We just studied each other, his brown eyes wild and scared, until the lids slowly drooped and his gaze seemed slightly softer.

It didn't bite me when I scooped it up in the snuggle and nestled it close to my chest. I rode my bike to the highway and started up the logging road. The coyote didn't fight, only growled a little when the road got rough and I jarred it too much.

"Tully?" I broke into the clearing, soaked and sweating. The animals, if they were there, were hiding from the rain. It poured through the thick tree canopy, splashing and clapping against leaves in a frantic percussion. There was no smoke coming from the little hut.

"Tully, I need your help." I assumed Tully was his name, the way he spoke when we first met. The yearling deer was almost a buck now. It stood up in the shadow of the opening to the hut and showed a spotless coat and antlers worn free of velvet. It stepped into the rain as I moved toward the door. I walked into a wall of stench: a coppery, acrid smell that clenched my gut.

It was dark inside the hut but I could make out two shapes. The first shape was the ghost bear curled with its head on its paws. The second shape was the man, Tully, sprawled out on the floor. His skin was loose and fallen in against the bones. An old revolver lay beside him where it had been dropped. He'd shot himself. His head was a mess, but the bear had left the body alone.

Outside, I retched and gasped. The buck looked up from chewing a horsetail stem. Somewhere, hidden in the ferns and tree trunks, one of the peacocks wailed a terrible song. The bear was asleep and I didn't want to see it awake.

I was just about to disappear into the bush when I heard the sparrow hawk. He called to me from above the trees, repeating the same question four times, then spun down through the tall columns and landed on an arm I didn't know I'd offered.

There was a leather tie around one of his talons. He blinked at me, then leaned his head to preen a wing feather. Carefully, slowly, I untied the leather strap on his foot, then tossed him up. He hovered slightly, the way an owl might pause mid-air, then disappeared above me.

The coyote couldn't stay there. I'd wanted Tully to take it, nurse it to health, make it one of his friends. But without Tully I didn't know what to do. I couldn't take it back home and I couldn't leave it there. I started to tear through the wet bush while considering the choices. Dad would have saved himself the trouble of climbing up the river, avoided the corpse and mysterious bear, simply shot the coyote and gone on with his day. That would have been easier.

I considered sneaking back into the hut to steal the gun. But the bear could wake up. The gun might not work. I could find a boulder, one so big I could barely lift it, and that would be swift, and certain. But I anticipated the sickening sound of the boulder crushing bones and knew I wouldn't be able to do it.

When I got to the creek I had settled on my only option. The coyote wouldn't be able to swim and I was determined to do the right thing. Among the moss-covered boulders I kneeled to the rushing creek. The surface was pockmarked and dancing in the rain. I cradled the sling in my arm. He didn't bite me. He didn't howl.

I hadn't noticed he'd stopped moaning. He must have bled to death, or maybe suffocated, I couldn't tell. He'd died curled up against my chest.

I slipped the sling into a comfortable position and began to hike home. At the dam I was careful not to slip or jar the sling, sorry that I hadn't been that careful before. By the time I got to my bike, I wasn't even letting the coyote hang against me. I held him, both arms cradled under his bony body, water dripping through the material and my numb fingers.

At home I dropped my bike in the grass and took a shovel from the shed. With the drooping weight still hanging from my neck, I dug a grave at the base of the oak tree.

After I filled the hole back in, dropped the shovel and collapsed beside it, I heard a cry in the rain. It was the same song I'd heard up the mountain—the kee kee kee of the sparrow hawk. I squinted into the low cloud and saw a grey shadow circling above me.

He called to me again, but I didn't raise my arm. I didn't whistle him down.

hammersmith

The red pickup truck spat dust toward the clouds as it rounded the corner. It was six-thirty on a Friday night and I was waiting at the bottom of the driveway for Mr. Hammersmith to pick me up.

As soon as we'd moved to the island, my mother enlisted me in the Scout troop. My father had proudly signed for the hatchet, pocket knife and steel-toed boots, scrawling his signature over the Dry Goods tab sheet, telling everyone around the woodstove how his son was going to be a trained islander.

My boots were tightly laced and my pack's stiff canvas was new on my back. The drab olive knapsack held the essentials I'd been ordered to bring to my first meeting.

The truck didn't slow down. Dust looped and swirled behind it. I could make out the shadow of a man at the wheel and the rest of the cab was empty. Two boys were standing in the back of the truck with their arms stretched over the roof of the cab and the wind tossing their hair.

"Ruuuuunnnnn!" one screamed over the bite of tires against the dirt road. I didn't move. I could hear the groan of the engine gearing down and I shuffled to the side of the driveway to let him pull in. The truck slowed minutely, and as it cruised past, one of the standing passengers yelled again. "Start running!"

Hammersmith's grin flashed as he drove by. The boys in the back waved their arms, urging me toward them. I ran. My arms pumped as if I was trying to take off. Dust coated my throat and clouded my eyes. The truck slowed enough that I could almost catch it, almost, by running.

"The bag," one of the boys yelled. Both had released their hold on the truck's cab and were now below the wheel wells, gripping onto the sides and reaching past the lowered tailgate. I swung my backpack from my shoulders and tossed it up to the truck. The smaller boy grabbed it with one arm, the other holding white-knuckled to the side of the truck, and hooked a strap over his leg so it wouldn't roll loose.

"Grab hold," the larger boy cried, offering his outstretched arm. I could barely see him through the dust. But they had my pack, my hatchet and knife. There was no going home without them.

I forced a sprint from my burning legs and leapt. The long arm caught me and my chest thudded against cold metal. My feet kicked out in the air, one boot toe bouncing in the gravel. The two boys tugged at my arm until I was belly-down in the back of the truck, gasping and coughing up dirty spit.

"Next time, start running as soon as you see the truck," the larger boy ordered. He didn't say anything else as we rattled up the highway. Just past The Rock, we turned a corner to see a chubby kid sprinting alongside the road as fast as a terrier after a rat.

"You grab his pack," the smaller kid ordered. "Mike Harvey needs both of us to pull *him* up."

As Hammersmith drove past the running boy, a pack was launched into the box. I caught it and held on with both hands, which was poor form since nothing secured me in the back of the truck.

The others had the finer points worked out. The bigger boy offered his arm, bent at the elbow like a hook. The chubby boy, red-cheeked and jiggling, spun in a strange manoeuvre. He half turned and caught his own crooked arm into the one offered him. The force of their arms meeting, combined with the direction of the half-spin both pulled and spun him over the side and into the box. The smaller boy grabbed Harvey's feet and helped roll him in. Then, after coughing up dust and whacking his chest with his fist, the chubby kid looked me up and down.

"Who's the new kid?" he asked. "Hammersmith have to stop?"

One shrugged and the other shook his head. The chubby kid glared at me. "Yous lucky he didn't have to stop. There's hell to pay for that."

"Hold on!" the little one yelled. We turned ninety degrees, off the dirt road and onto the grown-in path up the mountain.

We were eight boys in total, each with a hatchet, backpack and pocket knife. I was the only one wearing the little yellow kerchief around my neck. We emptied out of the truck in the Masons Hall parking lot and were given two minutes to find a way inside the building, excluding the locked doors. Without much discussion, the boys formed a chain, scaled the side of the building, removed a bug screen from an attic window, and guided each other through. I was last, on the heels of the chubby kid, Mike Harvey.

"Yous gotta screw it back in," he hissed at me, while shuffling his knees across the attic. I went back and spun the screws into their places, loose, so they might be easily removed in the future. Then I scurried across the attic and dropped into the meeting room. The seven others were standing at attention in a circle around Hammersmith, who scowled.

A moment of silence stretched as he glared, first at the

group and then at me in particular. He was leaning on a thick, brightly polished, shoulder-high walking stick.

"Six feet up!" he screamed. He banged the bottom of the stick against the wood floor to punctuate.

The rest of the group dropped their packs and scaled the walls and rafters as if gravity didn't apply. Hammersmith began madly swinging his stick, lifting his arm and swirling it through the air, hitting whatever he could reach.

I was slow. Anything or anyone found lower than six feet would be hit with the stick, starting from when Hammersmith made the announcement and ending when there was nothing left to hit. It was the second rule I learned in boy scouts—to always look for higher ground.

The first rule was to start running.

"How was it, Michael?" my mother asked anxiously. The house was dense with the smell of fresh cookies, which were cooling on a rack beside the stove. I dropped my pack and began to unlace my boots.

"Crazy," I said, and sighed. The living room walls flickered from my dad's late night news. "I didn't even learn anyone's names."

"I'm sure you'll make friends next week." She poured a glass of milk and passed it to me.

I tugged the yellow scarf off my neck and tossed it on the floor.

"You know, Mom, it's not like I don't know how to start a fire or use a hatchet."

She giggled and held one finger to her lips. "You'll have fun, just give it some time."

I considered telling her about the polished walking stick.

The second Scout meeting began with us standing around

Hammersmith, outside the wooden shack that was town hall. I got a few introductions. The tall, muscled kid was Thomas. The little guy was Mike Stubbs. When high school started in September, we'd be in grade eight together.

Hammersmith jolted us out of our little conversations with a quiz.

"What's a C.F.A., men?" He never called us boys.

"Come From Away, sir!"

"Stubbs, name three ways to tell a CFA."

"No flannel, no boots, no rust, sir!"

"Harvey, what's the best way to disarm a C.F.A.?"

"Using I.I., sir."

Hammersmith nodded and folded his hands into the crook of his armpits. He stared down at me. "And new one, Goldman, what's I. I.?"

I gulped. "What a ship's crew says to the captain?"

The group laughed but Hammersmith didn't even smirk.

"Inaccurate Information," he scolded.

The smallest Mike leaned toward me. "Good guess, though."

The door to the wooden building opened and Mr. Harvey, who ran the gas station uptown, waved us in. "We're waiting for yous in here."

Hammersmith called a forward march and we stomped inside to the front of the horseshoe table with town council sitting behind it.

"Tobias," the balding man at the head of the table called. "Looks like a good group here."

Hammersmith nodded.

"As many as last year?"

"Two more."

"And what about Salinger's son, Kris, how did his break heal?"

"Well."

"Good, good. Well, boys..." The man stood and patted his round middle. He skirted the table and stood in front of me.

"Who have we got here?"

"Mike Goldman, sir!" I answered. He stuck out his hand.

"Pleased to meet you, Mike Goldman. You must be new to the island. Where'd you come from?"

"Washington State, Mr. Mayor."

"Just call me Danny." He wheezed with each sentence. "Everyone does. So, an American. Your dad new to the quarry? Oh yes, Goldman...he's the new manager they got down there."

I could see the other boys elbowing each other. The mayor looked at Hammersmith. "You sure you want a newbie on this one?"

Hammersmith nodded. "He'll be an islander before the summer's over."

"Good, well, good then. You boys have fun."

We marched back into the parking lot.

"Six feet up!" Hammersmith screamed. We scattered, leaping into the trees.

When he stopped swinging his walking stick and it was safe to come down, we congregated around Hammersmith's dented truck. The box was full of street signs.

"Public service, men. It's the highest calling." He got in the truck and began a slow roll down the hill, toward the wharf where the ferry docked. The rest of us walked behind. The truck stopped in front of the large wooden salmon sign that read "Welcome to Smokecrest." Underneath the belly of the carved fish were arrows and hand-lettered notices advertising The Welcome Inn, The General Store, The Good n' Cheap, Harvey's Gas and The Pit.

Hammersmith threw a wrench onto the road. "Take 'em down, men."

Thomas picked up the wrench and Mike Harvey grabbed a hammer that landed at his feet. One by one, they removed all the small hand-lettered signs with arrows on them.

Ralphie climbed into the box and rummaged through the stack of professionally lettered metal signs that we'd driven from town hall. Bart passed the signs to me and I passed them to Kyle, who passed them to Thomas and Harvey, who nailed them up.

The wooden sign with an arrow that read "The Pit Café, get it while it's hot" was replaced with "Dining establishment. 1 km. Granite Ridge Road."

Then we drove around town and removed all the street signs.

"Why are we doing this?" I whispered to Mike Harvey.

"I.I., remember? It's so's the tourists don't find nothing."

"How was it, honey?" My mom was on her knees on the landing at the front door, scrubbing the clear vinyl runner that cut a path over the cream carpet. I sat on the step beside her and concentrated on my laces.

"Do you ever get the impression that people here don't like us?"

Mom put down her brush. "No, I never do. Why would you think that?"

"We're newbies."

"True. But we've lived in small towns before. We've lived in quarry towns before."

"They call us C.F.A.s."

"Do I want to know what that means?"

"Come From Aways."

"What's so bad about that?"

"Islanders don't like C.F.A.s."

She dried her hands on the legs of her jeans and sat up. "I know this isn't easy for you. It's not easy on your father or me either. He's got to come to a new place and be the boss and I've got to figure out how to deal with this monstrosity." She waved her arms around to indicate the house, which was an old brick and granite building that the mill managers had lived in since the quarry opened. It felt like a museum and my mother had been scraping, scrubbing, painting and redecorating since the day we moved in.

"But there are some good things about this place," she tried.

"Like what?"

"Well, first there's this Scout troop you're in, and that's a new adventure, isn't it?"

I snorted. "Yeah, if I survive."

"And it's a nice, small, safe little island. You can hike and fish and your dad's been talking about getting a boat."

"I like the island just fine, Mom. I'm not talking about the island. I'm talking about the islanders. They're weird and they don't like new people."

"Remember a few weeks ago when we went to the cemetery by the creek?"

"What about it?"

"What were some of the names that you saw over and over?"

I shrugged. "I don't know. Harvey. Dick. Louch. Hope. Swaney. There were lots of those."

"Right. And are there any Harvey, Dick, Louch, Hope or Swaney boys in your Scout group?"

I nodded. She patted my head. "Those are the families that have lived on Smokecrest for a long time. But you know what? All of them were, at one time, C.F.A.s. All of them except the Dicks, and they had different names then anyway. My point is that, eventually, you're gonna fit right in and no one will be able to tell you from another islander."

I shrugged and went to my room, annoyed. I considered

what made Islanders different. They don't come to a complete stop at stop signs. They don't have lawns. Islanders don't lock their houses or their cars or their businesses. When they walk their dogs, Islanders carry the unattached leash in their hands and let the dog run free. Islanders get their mail even if the address is wrong. Islanders never use cash—that's what accounts are for.

As I lay in bed and tried to remember my visit to the cemetery a pleasant thought arrived. In the clutter of that colourful graveyard, with its murals and flowers and prized collections, there had been a lot of familiar names, but no Hammersmiths.

Hammersmith tightened the red bandana around my eyes.

"Can you see anything?"

"No, sir."

"Good. Up you go."

He placed both my hands on the ladder rails that leaned against the branchless trunk of a fir tree. The tree was so tall it made the ladder seem small, but I was up four storeys when there were no more rungs to climb.

I turned around as I was supposed to, shuffling my boots and squeezing my eyes so tight a blindfold wasn't needed.

"Now, jump," he ordered from below.

"Jump. Jump. Jump!" came the chorus from the rest of the guys. At least I knew they were still there. On the ground, earlier, Hammersmith had explained that every new Scout did "the fire drill." The blindfold was "to instill trust."

My mouth was dry and my fingers ached from the death lock I had on the ladder.

"Jump, Goldman!" Hammersmith barked. I was sweating so much I thought I might slip. The ladder suddenly started shaking. Someone down below, someone strong, was shaking it side to side. I leapt. If Hammersmith happened to kill me, I had the small satisfaction of knowing my father would sue.

I pulled my legs into a front pike position in the air, as I'd been told. The bottom edge of the blindfold lifted and there was a blur of dark green. The troop groaned and shouted as I hit the canvas. The circular frame fell from their seven pairs of hands and the fringe of springs collapsed against the ground. I bounced up and down slightly. The group cheered and I pulled off the blindfold. Hammersmith was almost smiling.

"Not everyone makes it the first time," Harvey whispered as I climbed past him. "Most newbies stay up there crying until Hammersmith guides 'em down."

"God, I thought you meant no one ever survives."

"Oh, yous survive. Some just get a little hurt, that's all."

"You did what?"

"It was great. I jumped and they caught me. It was unbelievable."

My mother shut off the TV. "Mike, you could have been seriously injured."

"Nah, it's safe. We wouldn't do it if it wasn't."

"I think I'm going to have a talk with Tobias Hammersmith. What kind of man blindfolds a bunch of boys and has them jump from a ladder?"

"It was fun. Really, Mom."

"You didn't join Scouts to get yourself killed."

"It was fine. Really. Maybe I shouldn't have told you."

My dad lowered his book. "Relax, Rita. Tobias Hammersmith's a hell of a man. From what I heard, he came back from that war with more than one piece of metal in him. Everyone around here respects him. If he wants to teach a bunch of kids how to roll around in the woods, he's the right one for it."

"He's totally crazy."

I patted my mom on the arm. "True, but it's not so bad."

She flicked the TV back on.

"By the way, mom, we're going on a hiking trip next week-end, an overnighter."

"You're not going," she said, crossing her arms.

"Relax, woman," my father said with a sigh. "Let him be."

It didn't take me long to realize that C.F.As, or city folk, don't wear gumboots. Their shoes always look shiny and new. They don't smile when you walk past them on the docks. They drive cars, not trucks, which are always rust-free and clean. The men don't have beards and the women wear makeup. Their voices are always a little too loud and they're always in a hurry. They name their properties and call their new houses cottages. But the easiest, sure-fire way to tell C.F.A.s is to look at their wrists. Islanders never wear watches.

We sat on the beach beside the two canoes, weaving sinew around bent wood frames. Kyle Dick stood over us, giving instructions and occasionally farting to make us laugh. The smooth, round stones were agony to sit on and with the sun starting its slow decline, the breeze off the water was chilly. Hammersmith wouldn't let us light a fire, though. He said there was no time. None of us had eaten since lunch, and Hammersmith said we would do a cook-up after we set camp.

When we'd all finished our craft project, Hammersmith told us to load into the canoes. We split into two groups, four boys in each canoe and Hammersmith in his half-sized dory.

"Sir, there are no paddles," Bart announced.

"There are no paddles, sir," Ralphie said.

Hammersmith shrugged. I jumped out of the canoe with

everyone else and sprinted along the beach searching eagle-eye for a stick that was wide enough to pull water and smooth enough not to leave splinters.

Back in our boats, Hammersmith led the way, rowing in front of us so he was always watching. By the time we reached the gap between the islands, the sky was a deep blue with purple bands wrapped over the mountains on the horizon.

"Hold up," Hammersmith called. We stopped and he pulled his oars a few times to break away. Then he leaned over and fiddled with something at his feet. After a moment, he straightened up and tossed a fishing line into the water. He fixed the handle of the rod between his knees, and started rowing again.

"Not even," whispered Kyle.

The ocean was flat except for the occasional splash of minnows jumping. The lights of Smokecrest looked small and dreamlike from the water, as if the place were a wavy mirage. The island we were heading towards, Hood Island, with the singular geographical statement of Hood Peak rising almost straight up out of the water, loomed white-tipped like a grey-haired teacher.

We passed a cluster of granite islets and sent dozens of fat seals rolling off the bald rocks. In the water they studied us, some coming so close to the canoes I could see their brown puppy eyes in the dusk. One bumped our canoe slightly. The four of us yelled and the surrounding seals submerged.

As we pulled away, finally within reasonable distance of our landing beach, the seals launched themselves back onto the rocks, snorting loudly.

Hammersmith reeled in his line with nothing on the end.

"He's just suffering," Kyle quietly teased. It was rare to see Hammersmith do anything wrong.

"Too close to the seal rock," muttered Thomas.

We beached our little canoes and dragged them over the

waist-high boulders. It wasn't a good location for camping and we all knew Hammersmith wouldn't have made us build snow-shoes if we weren't going to need them.

"We go up, men," he ordered sternly.

Hammersmith had a small kerosene lantern that he held up at the front of the path, and we chugged up the Peak like a steam train going through the world's longest tunnel.

The air was cold but the steady incline kept us warm, and by the time we got to the first dusting of snow, we were shedding layers. When the snow got too deep, with a crusty layer that sometimes would hold and sometimes would give out and drop us through, Hammersmith stopped and had Kyle show us how to strap the snowshoes to our boots.

Harlan Manson's pair hadn't been lashed together tight enough and snapped undone like a spring the first step he took. Mike Harvey's weren't big enough to support his weight, and he sank through with the snowshoes on, as if he had giant potato mashers attached to his ankles. Hammersmith didn't bother. He was bigger than us and our waist-high only came up to his knees. The rest of us moved delicately over the crusted white surface.

By the time we got to the cabin we were falling-down hungry. It must have been well past midnight, and even on the exposed granite crest, looking over the tops of our island and all the surrounding islands and the glowing city beyond, there was no moon.

"Fry up," Hammersmith instructed as we all dropped our packs at the base of the rotted-out cabin stairs.

We cleared snow away with our hatchets and built a fire big enough for the nine of us.

"Usually he makes us build tents out of branches," Thomas said through a mouthful of beans. But that night we didn't bother with shelter. We spread cedar branches over the snow, rolled our sleeping bags out, and woke with the birds.

"Kitchen sink!" Harlan called. The cabin was close to falling in, the brick chimney laid down so long ago that moss blanketed the places where there was no snow. The roof had caved and I marvelled that someone had built this place, cleared the space and carried the bricks, only to abandon it and let it rot back into the wild.

Hammersmith had instructed us not to go into the cabin. So when he went for what he called "his daily," Harlan tiptoed up the soft stairs. Then he appeared triumphant in the doorframe, announced his find, and tossed the porcelain shell at our feet.

"Who's first?" Harlan threw himself from the top step and rolled in the snow. Thomas nodded.

Harlan dragged the sink over the crusty snow to the side of our camp that angled slowly downward, heading into the trail we'd climbed the night before.

"Just jump out when you want to stop, but hold on so it doesn't slide away," Harlan instructed, his eyes bright.

"Don't let it slide away," echoed Ralphie.

Thomas sat in the sink with his arms tight to the sides and his legs stuck up in front of him. Harlan rocked back and forth a few times, then pushed the sink forward as hard as he could.

"Kitchen siiiiiiiiiiink!" Thomas yelled cheerily, and he bounced down the snowy bank at a dangerous speed. A dock's length down the hill, the sink turned over and Thomas rolled to a stop, his laughter carrying up to the rest of us.

We cheered Thomas as he pulled the sink back up. Kyle guessed a seven between one and ten, and Harlan tossed his second rider over the snow.

Maybe it was the shape of the sink, with its slightly deepened bottom, that made it less like a sled and more like a rudder. Maybe it was the way Kyle was leaning. Whatever the reason, Kyle's path did not follow the safely worn trail Thomas had made. Kyle's sled veered in a surprising new direction. Kyle's sled was headed for the lip of the cliff.

There were all kinds of different screams and it was hard to make much out of any of them. I was yelling at Kyle to get off. Harlan was yelling at Jerry Swaney, who was standing by the campfire, to stop the sink. Kyle was just yelling.

Ralphie had gone to tend the fire, and when he looked over toward the yelling and saw Kyle getting quickly closer to the edge, he froze. In one hand he had a piece of half-split shingle he'd salvaged from the cabin. In the other hand he had his hatchet. It looked like he didn't know what to do.

"Stop the sink!" Thomas ordered. Kyle was almost past Ralphie. Ralphie lifted his arm. Just then, on the other side of Kyle, a head poked through the bushes. Hammersmith was a man of immediate action. He probably didn't even know what it was Kyle was riding in on his speeding trip to the Peak's ledge. It didn't matter. He'd launched himself into the air toward Kyle, faster than anyone—in particular, faster than Ralphie—could react.

At the same time that Hammersmith connected with Kyle, wrapping his huge arms around him and pushing them both to the snow, Ralphie let his arm go. He probably didn't mean to. It was probably just the surprise.

The sled continued on its path, hit the edge of the snowy rock and paused for a moment, frozen in the air, before gravity prevailed and it fell out of sight. Kyle and Hammersmith rolled in an intertwined ball away from the ledge and toward the campfire, and Ralphie's hatchet made a surprisingly loud "thwack" as it landed in a location two or three feet from the sink's path.

The rest of us ran toward the tumble of arms and legs on the ground, and as we got there, Kyle rolled free.

"Holy Christ Almighty," Kyle yelped.

Hammersmith sat up and looked at us. We all stopped.

"Do your best, men," he said severely. Then he fell back into the snow, the hatchet blade stiffly lodged in the side of his head.

"Don't touch him," Thomas ordered, offering Kyle a hand out of the snow and motioning us away from Hammersmith.

"Don't touch him, guys," squeaked Ralphie, although no one made any movement to suggest they were going to do such a thing.

Kyle stared at the ground. Ralphie looked as if he was about to cry. Mike Stubbs had his hand over his face. Thomas looked around, his face white, but after a long cold pause, he opened his mouth and spoke with authority. "We'll need to build a stretcher. Kyle, Ralphie, Stubbs, that's your job. Four handles for carrying. Long enough to support his head and his feet. Make sure it has support. Go."

Those three nodded and then tore off as Ralphie repeated, "Make sure it has support."

"Harlan, was there anything useful in the cabin?"

Harlan shrugged. "Like what?"

"Rope? Cloth? Canvas would be best. Any planking that's not rotten."

Harlan nodded. "I'll need a hand."

"Yep. Harvey, you go too."

Thomas looked at Bart and me. "Bring me the first aid kit and then pack up the whole camp. Hurry. Don't worry about whose stuff is whose."

I came back to Thomas, breathless, with the black aluminum

kit. Thomas opened it and pulled out a coil of bandage.

"You're not going to pull it out, are you?"

"No, that's what's stopping the bleeding." Thomas leaned over Hammersmith and gently wound the gauze around his head. "I want to keep it in place. It's going to be a rough trip down."

Harlan and Stubbs came back with some sturdy floorboards and some scraps of material that may have been sheets or drapes or towels at one time.

Bart was just finishing cramming the last few sleeping bags into packs when Kyle and Harvey came trotting out of the forest with the skeleton of a long stretcher.

"We need rope," Ralphie squeaked from behind them.

Harlan shrugged. "Couldn't find any."

"The sleeping bags then," Thomas directed. We demolished three nylon shells, lashed and secured the boards to the stretcher, while Thomas finished wrapping a strange turban of cloth around Hammersmith's head.

Starting at the feet, Harlan slid a smooth floorboard up Hammersmith's spine. The four closest boys transferred Hammersmith onto the stretcher. Thomas put his hands on his hips and let out a long sigh.

"This is going to be hard."

We all nodded. Some kicked at the snow.

"It's all downhill so we can go fast, but we can't run, it'll jar him. Most important is to keep him stable. He's floating down the mountain on a cloud of air. Got it?"

"Yes, sir!"

"We'll take turns. When you get tired, switch off. I don't want anyone tripping."

Harlan looked the stretcher up and down. "Then what do we do?"

"Yeah, then what do we do?"

"We'll figure it out on the way to the beach," Thomas muttered. "Hopefully we'll know when we get there."

If you figure that the birds start singing around four in the morning, just when the sun is thinking about pulling up, and water takes twenty minutes to boil, it couldn't have been much later than four-thirty that Hammersmith finished his coffee and went off into the bush. Harlan only spent a few minutes finding the sink and recruiting his first rider, so I figured Kyle was sliding toward the edge of the cliff by about five a.m.

The stretcher couldn't have taken more than twenty minutes to build, Hammersmith would have been proud of that. And so I guessed we were trotting down the trail off Hood Peak by about five-thirty. The sun was just hinting at heat and the trail was still dark.

We took turns carrying the stretcher and the extra packs and we talked between gasps about what we'd do next.

"We'll just row him to the island," Stubbs suggested.

Thomas shouted from the rear. "No good. Anything serious goes to the city."

"Yous want us to row him to the city?"

Kyle was in front of me, shaking his head. "Not even. It's way too long of a paddle to the city. It'd take half the day."

"It's a damn long paddle back to Smokecrest," Bart said with rare conviction.

"Yeah, damn long," agreed Ralphie.

We broke out of the trail to the boulder beach, where Hammersmith's dory and our small canoes waited upside down over wild rose bushes.

"Don't put him down," said Thomas as he tossed his two packs to the ground. Kyle and I stood at the edge of the path with the stretcher hanging at the height of our knees. The rest of the group pulled down the three boats. The water was still flat, which was crucial. A good chop and we wouldn't have been able to get Hammersmith off Hood Island.

Harlan filled the dory with all our packs and salvaged bits of rope from the three boats. As if they were pontoons, Harlan and Ralphie lashed the canoes to the sides of the dory in a way that had been decided coming down the peak.

"So, yous got a plan?" Mike Harvey asked. Thomas shrugged.

"Let's take him home," said Kyle. "At least Doc can look at him there before they take him to the city."

"Sure, but it's three, three-and-a-half hours home, and then yous have to get the doc, and then yous gotta put him on a ferry and take him to the hospital anyways," argued Harvey. "It's wasting a bunch of time."

Ralphie picked up a rock and skipped it on the flat water. "We don't want to waste time."

Bart waved his hands, oddly animated. "We've just carried him down the peak on no sleep and no breakfast. There's no way we can row him to the city."

Stubbs nodded. "That'd take even longer."

"Well, it's one or the other," Thomas barked.

"Maybe not," I said softly. "There's a third option."

Harlan came and took my end of the stretcher and I moved closer to the rest of the group.

"Look, Thomas, there's a ferry that leaves town at what, eight-twenty?"

He nodded.

"Eight-twenty," agreed Ralphie.

"So we paddle to the middle of the ferry route. It's on the other side of those islands, and it shouldn't take us more that two hours to get there."

"Then what?" Kyle asked.

"We signal the ferry, load him on, and he goes to the city," I said. "Captain'll have a radio. She can call for an ambulance. Plus we don't have to paddle as far, and we save Hammersmith a bunch of time."

There were smiles, but then Harlan argued. "It could work, but what if we get it wrong? What if we miss the middle point, or we get there and the ferry's already gone by? Then we've got more paddling or a long wait for the boat to come back. Besides, none of us knows what the hell time it is anyway, and if we don't know for sure, it's not worth the risk."

I kicked at a boulder. "I do."

Harlan blinked. "What?"

"Know what time it is."

Kyle squinted. "How?"

"How?" parroted Ralphie.

I shrugged. "I've got a watch."

They mumbled disapproval as I pulled the leather strap from my pocket. The face read 7:06. It was a birthday gift from my grandmother. I hadn't been able to get rid of it when I moved to the island.

Thomas leaned over and studied the watch face. Then he slapped me on the shoulder. "Great idea, Goldman. Load him up!"

I attached the band back on my wrist as the others gently secured the stretcher over the dory gunwales.

Using our driftwood paddles, we pulled through the water with surprising force. I was at the back of the canoe, constantly checking the time, and calling it out to the crew like a coxswain in a race.

At three minutes to nine, we arrived at the point we all thought to be exactly in the middle of the ferry's route. I announced the time proudly and the other boys cheered. Bart poured some water into Hammersmith's mouth. We prepared for rescue.

When the ferry was close enough in its approach that the captain, with her binoculars, would be able to see, Thomas gave orders. "Paddles in the air," he yelled.

We raised our arms and waved and in doing so quickly realized our problem. We didn't have paddles. We had driftwood. And although we were using them to pull ourselves through water, and although we were waving them in the air to indicate distress, it was clear even to us that no one was going to stop to help. We were eight boys in canoes waving sticks. We could very well have been playing pirates, kids from one of the summer camps out to torture the locals.

With the same sort of dreaded momentum that the sink had as it moved toward the edge of the peak, the ferry came forward. I knew, we all knew, there was only a small window before the boat passed by. I was not willing to let my plan fail.

"Cut the canoes free," I ordered.

"Not even," offered Kyle.

"Just do it," barked Thomas. Everyone on the insides of the canoes clicked open their pocket knives and cut the rope.

"Two men in the water," I yelled.

No one moved.

"Harvey, Stubbs, in the water!" cried Thomas. They rolled over the canoe edges and fell in head first.

"You guys take Hammersmith and keep him steady," I said. We pushed the dory out to the two treading water.

"Now quick, tie the canoes together again."

With the shortened bits of rope, Kyle and Ralphie tied us back into a raft.

"What's the plan?" Thomas asked, anxiously studying the dory with Hammersmith on top. Ralphie repeated him.

"Paddles in a pile in the middle of your canoe." Everyone followed. I grinned. "Now we light them on fire."

"The paddles are wet," said Harlan. But Thomas was looking to the ferry and then back to Hammersmith. He pulled out his waterproof matches. So did everyone else.

"Light the dry ends, then get in the water."

"Try not to splash," I added.

It took a few precious minutes for the canoes to really start smoking, but when they got going, they burned hot and fast. The eight of us bobbed in the water, each with one hand to steady Hammersmith. The burning canoes stopped the ferry and a rescue boat was quick to take us all in.

"Bravery," wheezed Mayor Hope, from the front of the hall, "is not something that can be taught, but something that simply is."

Thomas, Mike Stubbs, Mike Harvey, Kyle, Bart, Harlan, Ralphie and I had all been forced into suits and ties, and were seated in the front row, with most of the rest of the town behind us. Hammersmith was in a chair beside the podium, with one hand on his hip and the other grasping his whacking stick. The scar stretched across the left side of his face from his ear to the top of his forehead.

Since Hammersmith couldn't remember the specifics of the accident, meaning, he didn't know who'd thrown the hatchet, we decided not to tell him. It had become the best kept, and perhaps only, secret on the island. And because no one knew who'd caused the accident, we all got awards.

My name was the last one called.

"Some folks come to a place and never quite fit in," Hope said. "And then some folks come to a place and it's as if they've been there all along. This award goes to Michael Goldman on two counts. The first for bravery, with a dose of ingenuity added in. The second for darn good use of a wristwatch."

The hall laughed together and a few men called out, "Here, here."

Then we filed past the podium to shake hands and receive gifts. My dad was there to hand out new sleeping bags donated by the quarry. A stranger in a crisp uniform gave us special embossed Scout patches. Then we shook hands with Hammersmith, still seated in his chair. He smiled tightly and awarded each of us a waterproof wristwatch.

drinking herman dry

At first, my wife Nancy thought he was sweet.

"Poor old guy," she'd say when twice-widowed Herman Stubbs stood on his side of the fence watching us around the barbecue. "He must be lonely."

He no doubt was. But it got so we couldn't pull a weed or rake leaves or play horseshoes without Herman leaning toward us, watching it all. He was always home. And while he never actually crossed over the border, past the carefully stacked fence and into our barbecue dinners or our horseshoe games, he was close enough.

"Do you think that's why the Liebermans sold this place?" Nancy asked quietly. A friend had brought over a new strain of homegrown and we'd just stepped outside for an after-dinner smoke. Nancy and I were enjoying the fading September light and the smell of dry fir needles. Before we could even spark up, out came Herman in his slippers.

"Bonnie evening, auck?" Herman called, swirling his tumbler in his hand and folding his elbows over the fence. Nancy pretended to hear the phone ring and went back inside. She said Herman's fake accent drove her crazy.

"What time you be driving down-island tomorrow, Dennis?"

"Around eight. Why?"

"I've got to go down tomorrow; any chance you'd give an old goat a ride?"

I nodded. We talked about the weather.

When I went back into the house, Nancy couldn't believe we had no place to smoke.

"We bought a place so we wouldn't have to sneak around like teenagers, Dennis. This is insane."

"He's getting a ride with me in the morning, so you'll be free to light up in your yard all you want. Hell, dance naked, no one will mind."

Nancy huffed and rolled her shoulders back. "See, not even enough notice. I've wanted to have a garden party all summer. Finally he goes out and I only get ten hours notice."

"Go ahead and have your party, Nance. He won't bother you. He'll just stand there and smile. Probably do him some good to see a yard full of ladies."

Nancy smacked my arm. "He'd probably be standing there with an old boner, all those women in my yard."

"Good thing the fence is high." She smacked me again.

We ended up toking in the upstairs bathroom with the door shut and the lights off.

"Where can I drop ya, Herman?" He was sitting quietly in my boss's Rolls, filling the front with the antiseptic smell of booze breathing through skin. He'd just finished telling me about a civet cat he had living under his house, scratching away and smelling up his yard.

"Around that wee park in front of the doc's office. The one with that totem pole. Drop me off there. I've got people to see."

When I'd pulled over and Herman was about to shut the door, I asked, "When can I pick you up?"

"I'll be fine in a cab."

"That'll be quite the fare."

"Can I nay afford it?"

It didn't seem like Herman to snap like that.

I'd forgotten the appointment about the car. I had the frame of an old Cadillac in my garage that Nancy had been after me to sell. I'd always planned to fix 'er up, but the longer I held onto it, the less likely it seemed I'd get around to starting. So a week back I'd put an ad in the paper and taken some calls. Nancy and I were in the upstairs bathroom, at the back of the house, having a toke. We didn't hear a car pull into the driveway. We didn't hear the doorbell.

"Knock all ye want," we heard Herman call over the fence. "They won't hear ye."

"Nobody's home?" a strange voice asked. I leaned down and peered out of the window crack.

"Oh, they're home alright, but won't hear ye. They're up in that on-sweet, smoking the weed."

Nancy pushed me aside and slid the window open.

"What kind of weirdo are you, Herman, keeping track of what room we're in?"

Herman cackled and emptied his glass. I went down and practically gave the Cadillac away.

"Quite the neighbour you got there," the visitor said.

It cost a fortune in new window treatments. Nancy became obsessed with keeping all the doors and windows locked. One afternoon when I'd finished a job early and came home for lunch, I couldn't get in.

The windows were tight, the doors secure. I could hear her music turned up but couldn't see through to what room she was in because of the fancy blinds.

"Come on over," Herman called from his open back door. I figured I could at least call Nancy from Herman's and tell her to let me the hell in.

"Sandwich?" Herman opened his fridge and took out a pre-made, pre-cut sandwich on a china plate. He peeled off the plastic wrap and handed it to me.

"Scotch?" He already had a second glass poured and placed it on a coaster as he asked. I don't know why I was surprised at how nice his house was. The pillows on the couch looked fluffy and precisely placed. The carpet wore the tracks of recent vacuuming. Pictures hung even to the corners of the rooms. No scuffs on the walls, no clutter on the bookshelves. The kitchen smelled like lemons and the den was tobacco steeped.

"I've nay a few weeks," Herman said casually. "I can't tell my boys." I stopped chewing. "'Tis something I'll be needing your help with."

I nodded and emptied my glass. "What can I do?"

"To start you can bring over a wee bit of that reefer you pretend not to smoke. I've never tried it and I suppose it can't hurt now."

"Sure thing, Herman." I laughed, relieved his request was something I could manage. "When would you like?"

So that night, despite Nancy's insistence that I was about to walk into an RCMP snare, I knocked on Herman's back door with my tea tin inside my jacket.

"We'll start with the gentle stuff," I said, opening the tin and placing scissors, papers, and a couple of baggies on Herman's kitchen table. His eyes were as round as a pair of blue moons as I rolled the paper edges together and licked the seam. I passed it to him and he waved the wand under his nose like a gentleman offered a cigar.

"No, that's the filter," I stopped him. "Light the other end."

We sat at his kitchen table as the smoke swirled in the lamp light. There was a scratching against the floor.

"Dinna hear that?" he asked. "Damn civet cat. Ripping up my insulation."

"It won't do too much damage, will it?" I didn't hear anything.

"Stinks up the place like a rotting seal on the beach. Keeps me awake with scratching." Herman stood and disappeared for a moment. He came back with a shotgun.

"You can't shoot it, Herman. Put that away."

"Auck, I'll be needing your help."

He walked out his back door, both hands on the gun.

"Lift that open," Herman ordered. He kicked his foot in the direction of a hinged panel on the side of his house. I struggled with the rusted hinges but finally opened the door and looked into the dark crawlspace.

"There's nothing down there."

"Stand back."

"Come on, Herman, there's nothing down there. Let's at least get a flashlight."

But he'd already hunched over and was peering down the barrel.

"I can see the weasel's eye," he whispered, and blasted the shot into the empty crawlspace. Shaking his head as if he had water in his ears, Herman fell to the ground laughing. It was an undone, wild sort of laugh, contagious and oddly warming.

"You're crazy." I leaned down into the black opening. "There was nothing down there."

"Dinna say," Herman said sternly, rising from the grass.

And it turned out I was wrong. When we got a flashlight and I edged under the house to retrieve the body of the civet cat, I discovered that Herman had managed to hit something. He'd blown shot into his pipes. There was water everywhere.

"Damn it, Herman, I'm a chauffer, not a plumber."

We turned the water off and eventually ended up back at the kitchen table, finishing off a drink.

"Let's smoke another," Herman suggested.

"I'm not giving you any more. I've never seen anyone act so stupid."

"Don't be bowfin. Had nothing to do with your wacky tobaccy. I've been meaning to shoot that cat for months, I just couldna open the hinges."

I wouldn't share any more smoke but we drank for a while. Herman told his wild story: how he'd seen the glint in the civet cat's eye. He insisted that he'd absolutely killed the critter, but the burst pipes had washed the body away. I didn't get home until late and I was sure that this time Nancy had locked me out on purpose.

The next night Nancy and I smoked on the back step with Herman leaning over the fence.

"So then the one plumber's yelling 'Jesus God damn!' And I'm up in the living room trying not to snicker. Then the second plumber says, 'What? What the hell? I've never seen one of these...Manson...What the hell is this? And I'm thinking maybe I should have taken the quote and not the hourly rate. Then the first plumber says 'Please God, just a little help here, please?' It's nay good hearin' your plumbers ask for divine intervention."

We snickered and puffed smoke toward the trees. Nancy had been letting Herman use the downstairs washroom all day, after I'd promised her that no matter how old he was, he wasn't going to piss on her floor. I told her how Herman was the tidiest man I'd ever seen but Nancy said I wouldn't know tidy to look at it. His plumbing was fixed in a day, with all the pipes replaced, and Nancy was happy.

"When you're done with that, Dennis, would ya nay come over for a wee spell?"

Nancy gave me a look that said I was welcome to go over but if we shot anything else I might as well not come back.

When we were back at the kitchen table, Herman poured and considered his words.

"The doctors said two weeks, antha was a few weeks ago."

I nodded slowly.

"Now I don't mind, really. 'Tis true, I don't go out, can't work. Susan's been gone for years. And everyone else too. Both my kids are around but they're not the people to help me here. Nay family, auck. I'd do it on my own. Only problem is..."

I held in my breath.

"...I've gotta lot of booze."

I blinked.

"Back when I dinna know how long it would be, I stocked up. Practically bowled the store over with my order. But now, well, time's running out."

I still didn't understand.

"I don't mind the dying. 'Tis pretty much expected." He paused. "I just dinna want to go before I can drink it all."

I would have laughed except for Herman's countenance, which wore the chiseled lines of a serious man. He stood, took up his glass, and waved me closer with his other hand.

"Come with me," he said, leading me down the hall into his garage. The air was dry and smelled of dusty concrete. The garage had no vehicle.

"See these boxes?" he asked, pointing to a stack of cardboard squares up against the wall. "All scotch."

I buried my hands in my pockets and rocked my feet on the cold floor.

"Must have cost you a fortune."

"Worth it."

He waved me back into the house. "Now the help I'll be needing from you, Dennis, is to help me drink it."

"I don't know, Herman, that's a lot to drink. Nancy'd kill me for one thing, and my liver would probably do the same. Why don't I just take it back to the store? You could cash it in and do something nice for yourself."

"I did do something nice for myself. I bought the scotch. That's bran new, isn't it?" Then he put his hand on mine, the first time I could remember that we'd touched. He radiated warmth and it startled me.

"Promise you'll help me, Dennis. Promise we'll drink it before I go."

"What about your sons?" I tried, lamely.

"They dinna want to see their old man drink hisself to death, now do they?" I decided that Herman, crazy as he was, was probably right.

"I'll divorce you, is what I'll do." Nancy was making the bed, but at some point in the conversation her attempt at stuffing pillows into cases disintegrated into her mindlessly pounding them with her fist. "You've got a job. You've got obligations. I'm not going to stand for it."

"What are you trying to say, Nancy?"

"This is shit, Dennis. Just shit."

I took the tenderized pillow from her hands and made her sit on the edge of the bed. Then I sat down beside her. "You know I was up at camp when my grandfather died..."

"That's not relevant."

"I never got to the hospital in time to say goodbye to my dad..."

"It's a fool's errand. Do you even know what he's supposedly dying from? He's probably just making it all up, a good story to lure some soft-hearted sucker in."

"He made me promise."

"He's just a well-pickled old pervert. And the fact that he's interested in you and not me doesn't do a thing to ease my mind."

"So what's a few drinks with a dying man going to hurt?"

"You said it was an entire garage full of booze."

"A few boxes *in* the garage. That's different. And Herman will probably drink the majority."

"I'm not cleaning up any vomit."

I laughed.

"If you're hung over that's your problem. And if this affects life around the house, it's over, I don't care. I want the garbage out and the lawn mowed. You so much as miss a blade and I'll... well...I don't know what but I'll do it."

After a week of going to Herman's right after work, drinking into the evening and stumbling home, Nancy took her stand.

"Got a headache, do you?" She seemed to be clanking the pots and bowls extra loudly as she emptied the dishwasher.

"Jeez, Nance, could you take it easy?" I massaged my temples.

"I didn't think you'd actually go through with it. I can't stand it."

"What harm is it to you?"

"You're going to have to deal with him. You can't be over there every night. It'll kill you."

I nodded. I certainly hadn't drunk this much in my military days, and that was a long while ago, when I was in shape for it. "I'll work something out, honey," I offered. I blew against my coffee and the steam warmed my face.

Driving home from work on Friday afternoon, I noticed an un-usual number of cars in the Legion parking lot. Milling around in the misty rain was a group of men in beards and kilts. I pulled to the side of the road.

"Howdy, Angus." I slapped a broad shoulder. Angus Rose threw an arm around my neck and pulled me toward him.

"Grrrreat to see you, Dennis," he said, his tongue rolling in an exaggerated brogue.

"What's going on?" I asked. "Who are all these guys?" There were at least twenty faces I didn't recognize.

"These guys are the pipers. We had ourselves one fine old pipe-off. Our fellas didn't do so well but it was crackin' fun."

"Have you guys got plans for tonight?"

Angus shook his head. "Nothing in particular."

The mist had blown away and light radiated in bright shafts as the sun dipped below the clouds. Herman and I sat on his back porch with our feet up and our glasses full.

"Dinna hear that?" Herman asked, tilting his head to one side.

"What?"

"The pipes."

"You're having trouble with the new pipes?"

"No. Listen." Herman rose from his chair and took a step into the yard. "Pipes. Oh Danny boy, the pipes, the pipes they are a'calling."

The strangled cat wail of bagpipes came on the breeze from a distance. "Yeah, I hear it. Someone's TV is too loud."

"That's nay TV." Herman waved his arm, beckoning me out to the lawn. "Did I tell ye I used to play the pipes? Back when I was young, my grandmother tried to teach us all."

"I remember you said something like that."

"They're getting closer."

The sound was building. Instead of hearing one lonesome hum there was a chorus of pipes and even the rhythmic heartbeat of drums.

Herman walked around his house to the front yard and squinted up the street. I followed.

"It's coming from that direction," he predicted, pointing up the empty pavement.

We watched the distant corner as the music got louder. Then the Cross of Saint Andrew came into sight, carried by the first member of the long parade. The pipers marched in time to the drum. Other neighbours on the street opened their front doors and stood on their stoops, fists to hips, jaws open.

The company stopped in front of Herman's house, where the group turned in unison to face us on the lawn.

"Will ye no come back again," Herman said softly, after the band faded from one song and whined into another.

"I bet they're thirsty," Herman said. "It's thirsty work. Should I not invite them for a drink?"

The next morning I was back at the kitchen table with my head in my hands.

"All things considered," Nancy said softly, "It was a fun party." I was glad she'd had a good time, but she'd gone on to bed with the rest of the neighbours around midnight, long before the ceilidh really got going.

"So how did the fight start?"

"Angus made a toast to Herman. Then Harvey made a toast to the Queen. Then Blind Barry McDougall said 'Feck the Queen.' Angus jumped over the kitchen table and everyone started whomping on everyone else."

"And what exactly happened to my fence again?"

"Caber toss."

"The pieces are all over the yard."

"Don't worry, Nance. That's the beauty of split rail. I can

stack it all up again."

"And when did the ambulance come?"

"After the fight."

"Did someone hit him?"

"Nope. He was laughing when he collapsed."

Nancy put her hand over mine. "I'm glad you called the Stubbs boys."

"You know what he said in the ambulance, Nance? He put his hand on his heart, and smiled. He said, 'Dennis, I'm right peaked we had the wake first. That's the way it oughta be.' He said some things to his sons. He told me to make the tombstone out of the empty bottles, then he went."

"And you managed to drink it all?"

"Every last drop."

Nancy raised her coffee mug. "Well, here's to Herman, that old fart."

"Cheers, honey," I said, and Nancy started to cry.

devil hunting

There's never much to do around here on a Friday night. Welcome to Nowhere should be the town motto, painted under the arching belly of the salmon carved into the tall wooden sign at the town limits. Our town may be called Smokecrest, but it's actually Nowhere.

My mother has different sayings and it all depends on the circumstances, which one I get. Some days, when it's raining and dull and I'm bored and flopping around on the sofa, she will say, "You have to make your own fun."

Then I hear about her and her seven brothers staging plays and jumping from pieces of ice floe for a good time. And before going to my room to sulk, I remind her I'm an only child, living in a temperate climate, where there is no ice floe to amuse me.

Another saying, which she saves for Fridays after school, like today, is that, "As your mother I have every right to know where you are, and what you're doing." Which is invasive but comical at the same time. It's Smokecrest; if anyone is really worried all they have to do is climb to the top of the bluff and look down. We're on a damn island and there's only one road. But she still likes to warn against things. She says, "You shouldn't go borrowing trouble, not even in Smokecrest."

Of course I was born here; that's a major source of embarrassment for any Smokecrest teen. When I'm in the city for a day, and asked where I was born, I say "Smokecrest."

And they say, "Where?"

And I say, "Smokecrest, it's an island near the city."

And they say, "Oh, do you have electricity there?"

I don't tell them exactly where I was born, because no one believes me anyway. City people don't believe that babies are still born in longhouses. Being white doesn't help my tale, either. City people don't believe in things like well water, or oil lamps, or only having one road. How do you explain survival tools to city folk? How do you explain island magic? I don't even try.

I meet Thomas on the beach with a duffel bag over my shoulder and a small cooler in my hand. The boat is full of teens without lifejackets, so he brings it in slow. Usually Thomas guns the motor before hitting the switch to lift the propeller leg, then the boat coasts to the beach with momentum. But today he lifts the leg early because the boat's weighed down and floating low in the water. Thomas passes a pike pole to Harlan on one side of the boat, takes one for himself, and together they pull the aluminum workboat in as if it's a gondola in Venice.

Thomas has a stereo rigged onto the dash because he never goes anywhere without loud music. I can see an older pair of islanders sitting on a log up the beach, Harriet Hope and her son Danny, shaking their heads at our commotion. My mother will hear about this.

Harlan takes the duffel bag from my shoulder, then Thomas reaches over the side and hooks his hands under my armpits, hauling me up like a child being pulled from the pool when the lifeguard blows the whistle. "Hey, Kitten," Thomas says. Everyone calls me Kitten now, not just Cat. Thomas started that.

Besides Thomas, Harlan, and me, there's Tricia, Mike

Stubbs, Mike Harvey, and Mike Goldman in the boat. My gear is tossed into the hollow hull, then two of the Mikes climb over the windshield to sit in the bow. Thomas throws them a rope to hold onto when we hit waves. Tricia takes the one free seat. Harlan and Mike Stubbs sit on the boat's side, holding cleats for support. I climb onto the fibreglass hood covering the engine, just to Thomas's left. It's a good place to sit because I can lean back against the tow post, and the engine keeps me warm. Sometimes the fibreglass makes my jeans itchy, but I can't be picky when I'm the last one onboard.

The Mikes use pike poles to push us away from the beach, and Thomas lowers the propeller leg. If we were in a car, we'd be burning rubber. Harlan yells above the engine noise, "What does the Devil like to drink?" and we all yell "Beer!" Then we laugh for minutes. We are a band of pirates without frilly shirts. One of the Mikes has a bandanna tied over his shaved skull. Harlan holds his pike pole like a staff, as if he were bringing commandments down a mountain. The Jolly Roger flies from the back of the tow post. We see no other boats out on the water.

To get hydroplaning, Thomas has us lean forward while he pushes the engine as hard as it will go; we slog through the chop until we pop up on top of it. Skimming the waves at full speed in the aluminum hull feels like riding a mechanical bull set to ten. Or how I imagine it would be, if I'd ever tried it.

Thomas has a girlfriend. I think about that every second. Thomas is not the kind of guy who goes around, single; that's not the way things work. It's funny how I never really noticed him for all the years we've been in school together. And then one day, I did.

His girlfriend's not allowed on this camping trip with us. Something about being grounded for breaking curfew. I'm not too worried about her, though. The Mikes don't like her. No one stays with Thomas long, if the Mikes don't approve, but the Mikes seem to like me, so I'm hopeful.

The tide is low when we pull into Lipton's Bay. The skeleton of a massive wooden ship is scattered down the length of the beach, poking out of the water like stripped trees after a flood. The ship ran aground with a full cargo of tea, a hundred years ago, back before the rocks and reefs were charted around here. The barnacle-covered bones of the ship are crowned in sea-weed; it's eerie and sad and reeks of the sea.

An eagle sits on a log floating just a few feet from where the ocean runs into land. I stare at it, amazed at how close it is. Then the eagle bends its head to its talons and there is a wet, ripping sound. The eagle sits up straight again, a patch of red flesh dangling from it's hooked beak. We all scream in disgust, but our noise doesn't scare the bird away. It's no log the eagle's perched on, but the bloated body of a dead seal. Which explains the smell.

Thomas brings the boat in past the wooden ship's ribs, past the eagle, and runs the hull up onto the rocky beach where the Mikes jump off, holding their ropes to pull us ashore. Up where the beach turns into dense fern cover, a moss-covered shack leans away from the ocean. It wasn't always a shack; once it was a two-storey house that watched the tall tea ships sail by. There's a strange feeling to the place, as if no one could ever really call it home. The old cabin roof is mostly fallen in, with thin alder trees grown up through the gaps.

Tricia and I gather boulders into a circle on the top of a smooth granite patch overlooking the beach. Mike Goldman uses his hatchet to hack down branches, and he quickly fash-ions an A-frame tent out of cedar boughs. "This is how we did it back in Nam," he teases. He's watched too many movies.

Beers are opened, passed around. Tricia and I wait patiently for the boys to gather wood for our fairy ring of stones. But before we have enough wood, Harlan takes a can of fire-starter, squirts it over the closest corner of the deteriorating shack, lights a match, and drops it.

It's easy to be carried along by events such as these. I felt tingly from the beer, equally drunk with a new sense of freedom, the feeling I had that Thomas was watching me, and the beauty of the sunrise slipping into twilight. Back in town, we'd never be so wild as to torch the old house on the farmland across the street from school. That would be arson, and asking for trouble. But out here, on the secret side, there's no parents, no principal, just three Mikes, Tricia, Thomas, Harlan, and me with a can of fire-starter and some matches.

We roast hot dogs, bracing ourselves against the scorching heat as we dart back and forth from the tall flames. It's the biggest fire I've ever seen. I don't ask, but I get the feeling everyone else feels the same awe.

Harlan finds some deer bones. Up through the bushes in the shadows of the burning cabin, he finds a deer graveyard, two full bony testaments to quadruped existence. The skeletons were probably left behind by hunters, but it's spooky, since we don't know for sure. The boys gather the bones and bring them down to the stone circle. Mike Harvey, acting a little drunk, takes a long straight branch and spears a deer skull so it's stuck in place. He waves the staff in the air so the skull circles high against the light of the fire.

Harlan does some sort of strange booty dance, chanting and grunting and bobbing around. The other boys pick up on it first, and they follow each other until they're all dancing together in a circle. Tricia howls with laughter, and clicks a few shots on her camera. The flash of light against the trees—that little bit of civilization thrown against the dancing—is unnerving. Mike

Stubbs picks up two long leg bones and uses them as drumsticks. Thomas jabs a leg bone into a chunk of burning wood and holds it up like a torch or a flaming baton. We dance around the stone circle, grunting and kicking, acting loose and lost. It feels like we are free. Finally free.

And that's when Thomas's radiophone rings. It's my mother, asking to speak to me.

My cheeks burn with shame as I lift the heavy receiver to my ear. "We're just on the far side of the island...Yes, Mother, we are fine...No, it's OK, I'm just sitting really close to the fire...Because it's cold outside! God, why else would you sit close to a fire?...Of course we'll put it out before we leave."

My jaw is clenched so tight it feels as if I might crack a tooth. She ruins everything. Why did she have to check on me? I let my cold anger pour through my voice as I say goodbye, hoping she'll hear it.

When I hand the phone back to Thomas, the group is quiet. They've dropped the bones and sit facing the fire, suddenly sober, caught at the end of our adventure by my mom. It's claustrophobic, knowing the size and circumference of an island so small. How had she known to call then, right when we'd gone just a little too far? You can't borrow trouble when you come from Smokecrest. With a mother like mine, you can't even try.

We form a fire brigade and use bail buckets from the boat to scoop seawater onto the house. The salt smell sizzles into the black sky. My arms ache from passing buckets before the flames have been extinguished, but with each pass of the bucket from Thomas, his fingers seem to stroke against mine. I can't take a break until I'm sure it's not accidental.

When everything is wet enough not to flare up again, and there is only one large charcoal scar marking our campsite, we pile the bones into the middle of the stone circle, and pack up the boat. We tell each other we're leaving because the washed-up dead seal smells too bad to sleep through, and that seems like as good a reason as any. No one mentions the phone call.

Thomas guides the boat slowly over the dark, choppy water. On a bump from a wave, his left hand casually falls over my right knee, and he holds it there, the rest of the way back.

None of our parents expect us home, but we all go there anyway.

eagle's nest

Will slapped a five-dollar bill against the dropped gate of the pickup truck. He hit it with enough force to knock over Ralphie's beer can.

"Ain't likely," Will said as Ralphie followed with his own fiver.

The men spat into their palms and squished out a hand-shake.

The five-dollar bet was for Eagle's Nest. The old pickup truck, the one Ralphie had bought up-island the day of his sixteenth birthday with money he'd made stacking dead batteries in the scrap yard, was idling on the flat at the top of the cliff. The headlights broke into the air above the water in parallel beams and shone out like a lighthouse eye rusted into place.

They'd both jumped off the lower-level Crow's Nest before. In the summertime the girls sunbathed down on the baby-jump level, while boys scaled the rock, wet and panting, to take a running leap from the middle-point of the granite face, then yell or hug into a cannon ball to make the girls scream.

Usually, as the summer faded into looming September, an adventurous few would climb up to the Eagle's Nest ledge and peer down at Crow's Nest below, while the ocean passed, almost unfathomably far beneath them. The kids on the beach would hold their hands above their eyes to block the sun, look up at the brave, half-naked figures and scream that the only way down was to jump.

Which was not true. Because every summer each climber came down by climbing, shamed, like a treed bear finally left to descend alone. No one could remember actually seeing anyone run along the short ledge, push off on the jagged tooth of stone that jutted out the farthest, kick through the air to clear Crow's Nest and jackknife into the water. But the myth persisted that someone, once, had done it, and someone might do it again.

It was the rock dust from work that led the bet. Ralphie brought Will and the whisky and the cans of Bud to the end of the cliff-top road to discuss Melanie, a flat-chested girl who had told the island that Ralphie was the father-to-be of what he imagined as the ugliest child ever.

"A little dirt won't kill ya," Ralphie said. He fitted an empty beer can into the "v" between his forearm and biceps. Then he flexed slowly until the can crumpled. There was no one around to be impressed by this, but Ralphie liked to keep in practice.

"I can't stand the rock dust," said Will as he reached back to take another can from the cooler tied into the truck box. "The best part of my day is getting home, hopping in the shower, and scrubbing all that crap off. Sometimes if I'm still hot, I'll just use cold water. But man, it feels good, getting clean."

"You're a loser," Ralphie said profoundly. He never considered what a shower felt like. He cleaned up after work like everyone else, but it never occurred to him to enjoy it.

Will argued, "You don't feel nothing, man."

Ralphie grabbed his crotch and shook it as if he was meeting someone new. "I feel this."

"Yeah, you feel that too much."

Ralphie was suddenly reminded of Melanie, and the reason he'd brought Will up here, but he didn't want to talk about it right away. So he mentioned the water.

"Why don't you go for a swim? That'd clean you up."

"Too cold." It was warm and they both knew it. "So I hear a rumour going around," Will said casually, "about you and some girl."

"Bet you can't jump off Eagle's Nest," Ralphie dared. It was true that he wanted to know what Will thought, and it might even have been true that he'd knocked the girl up, but suddenly he didn't want to hear about it.

"I don't want to jump off Eagle's Nest," said Will.

"Chicken."

"You know I could if I wanted, but I don't want to."

"Come on, the water's not that cold. You'll get all cleaned up the way you like."

"I thought you wanted to talk about the girl."

"What's to talk about? Come on, I betcha five bucks you don't jump."

"You jump."

Ralphie shrugged. "I'm not gonna if you don't."

"I'm not jumping first 'cause I know you. You'll just stay up here and laugh."

"Fine, I'll go first but only because you're a chicken who can't trust his buddy besides." Ralphie bent over and untied his steel-toed boots. He didn't want to jump and couldn't imagine why he was going to. It was all because of the girl. He hated her so much he'd rather jump off a black cliff than talk about her. But Will was a good friend, and he knew all this, and he wouldn't let Ralphie get away with it.

"So, about those rumours," Will tried again as he swigged at the whisky bottle and kicked away one of the discarded boots.

"Yeah," Ralphie sighed and rolled his toes into the rock. "I been meanin' to talk to you about them."

"Well, you're gonna marry her, right?"

"Whaddya mean? I ain't marryin' no pointy-nosed, flat-chested, little nothin' like her. Besides, you don't think I'm the dad, do you?"

Will shrugged. "You always said she was frigid."

"Exactly." Ralphie crushed another beer can and chucked it so it rattled down the rock face. "See, she never let me into her pants back when I was interested in 'em, you know? And now I'm not interested no more, she's spoutin' I knocked her up."

"But you were interested."

"Once."

"And you did try to get with her."

"Way back a time."

"But you don't think you're the dad?"

Ralphie sighed. "I don't think I am, but I was hopin', maybe, you know, you might be able to tell me."

"Tell you what?"

"Well, did I get with her or not?"

Will laughed.

"No, seriously, man." Ralphie's voice squeaked. "You'd know, right? I mean, was there one of those parties a few months back where maybe I got with her but don't remember?"

"Every party we go to, you make up a story about getting with one girl or another."

"They're not all made up."

Will replied with a punch to Ralphie's shoulder.

"But you see the deal, right? I mean, did I get with her or didn't I? If I did, I s'pose I got some responsibilities. But if I didn't, well, phew, I just escaped by the hairs on my ass, ya know?"

A loon called out from the black water below. Ralphie fingered the loose denim threads blooming around a hole in the thigh of his acid-washed work jeans.

"She's a nice girl," Will said quietly.

"If ya think so, why don't you marry her?"

"She's not in love with me."

"Not even."

"Seriously, Ralphie. She's crazy about you. You spent so much time bugging her, trying to make it with her, that she fell for it. Now suddenly you're not interested. It makes me think—"

"That's a dangerous sport."

Will ignored him. "It just makes me wonder. I mean, suddenly you stopped chasing her. And if you do the math, backwards I mean, it sort of makes sense."

"Well, I don't remember nothin'," Ralphie said stiffly. "That's why I need you. You tell me what to do and I'll do it and that'll be that."

"I don't know, man," Will said sincerely.

It was the hopelessness in Will's voice that made Ralphie edgy.

"So are we jumpin' or not?" Ralphie didn't like talking about the girl and he didn't like the tone his buddy was taking on the topic. Best to ignore it, have a beer, feel the cold crush of the ocean.

"You got five bucks or what?"

Will laughed and Ralphie could tell he was plastered from the way it rolled on too long.

"Maybe I'm not the father," Ralphie said hopefully. Will fumbled for his wallet.

"This town is crap with all its expectations. She doesn't even have to have it, ya know? Probably some other guy will come forward, ya know, fess up to it, marry her, raise the kid. "

"Ain't likely," Will said, slapping a five-dollar bill against the dropped tailgate and knocking over Ralph's beer can.

Ralphie followed with his own fiver. "You go first, man, and

I'll be right behind ya."

Will removed his work boots and took a run off Eagle's Nest. In the headlights of the truck, Ralphie saw Will kick through the black air before disappearing into it. After a godless moment, there came the distant splash of water. Ralphie waited to hear Will call up, or laugh. When he heard nothing, Ralphie did what was expected of him. He broke into a sprint and jumped.

free is free

I got so much trouble on my mind. Blood visions of plaintive women. Paper money fluttering through the air. That sound, that smell. Hand-shined chrome meeting venerable old-growth trunk, the moss wet, the road reeking of molten rubber, the tires drawing protest all the way to the edge.

It's raining. Hasn't broke loose and rained in months, feels like, and my skin is dry, cracked, hot like the road-side grass; evaporates any moisture that falls to it. There's nothing left to do but walk. You ditch the car, you walk away. That's the way it's always been done.

The sign reads "Four Dancers To Nite" with a shattered hole in the middle of the luminescent message: a rock, catapulted from the back of a flat deck one early dewy morning. Four dancers start at seven p.m. It's now at least midnight, which means each of those women musta come out, taken it off, put it back on and then peeled again, late night left for when the men are too tired, too drunk to remember.

I always remember. Don't mind the bodies on repeat; a body's a body. But these girls have a limited repertoire. They dance to the same songs. How many times can a man hear "Mustang Sally" in a night? Must be weird for them, seeing us at the grocery store, the dry goods, and us not meeting their eyes, pumping their cars with regular, them always naked, always puckered and jiggling in the front of our brains. Some of them offering a rub and tug in the back parking lot. Some of them married with children, if you can believe that.

The stage is immediately to the right of the front door which means I get an ass in my face when I walk in and I've seen that ass before. I do my best not to smack it, get a laugh from the crowd. She's dancing to "Hard Day's Night." The bartender is a toothless hag who wears a jack shirt unbuttoned to a whirlpool of cleavage that sucks you in. You don't want to look but you can't help it. She's draining a keg of Blue when I take a stool.

"Crashed my car."

She fills a glass with the beer dregs and slides it over in sympathy. It's flat but free is free. I drain the heavy glass in two gulps. She slides down a pissy pitcher. I nod in appreciation and turn away to study things. It's the kind of place that needs to be kept dark. Wood-beam ceiling cloistered in years of cobwebs and dust never cleaned. Burned-out bare bulbs. A pool table scarred with cigarette burn hieroglyphics. Ash on the floor. The last place on earth you can smoke inside, in any room.

I keep my hat low despite the need to scratch, to throw it on the lino'd bar and run both hands over my head. I hang over my drink and think for a minute. I always need to think for a minute, but that minute doesn't come. I pound a fist down and it feels good, the curl of fingers, the jolt up to my elbow.

"Got trouble?"

I've seen this guy before, crater-faced soul-sucker. He's eyeing my pitcher, doesn't see it's flat. He's big though and I don't like that. Don't like the big guys eyeing my pitcher. I motion for another glass. Free is free.

"You get more than your money's worth with that one," crater-face says, lowering to the stool beside me, slow and pained, like he's got prostate trouble. He thanks me for the beer, then squints his eyes after the first thirsty drink.

A group of kids come in, their sleeves rolled up and their hats annoyingly asymmetrical on their heads. The stage is empty now and the square, seventies jukebox clicks back in. No neon or shiny bubbles, looks more like a cigarette machine. Damn tough though, utilitarian, made it this long. One of the boys goes straight to the jukebox. Kid's taking his life in his hands, doesn't even know it. A tension mounts in the room as he rattles his coins.

His buddies at the bar are busy getting long-necks of some over-priced swill with two Xs on the label. Fag beer, but they're all drinking it. They have no idea. Kid presses a button and Gram Parsons and Emmylou Harris start singing how love hurts. Every soul in the room understands. An old-timer slaps the kid on the back as he walks by, oblivious to the test he just narrowly passed.

The boys go to the pool table. Crater-face and I finish the pitcher. I order myself a whisky and pay for it, tip for the beer. Crater-face is on his own.

The ass I met at the door appears from the back room, only it's jean-clad now. She's pretty. Paula. Paulette. Something like that. Long, artificially yellow hair in a shaggy wave. She's wearing flip-flops, a t-shirt, no bra. Somehow this seems indecent, to go back, get dressed, and come out with perky tits under a thin layer of cotton. What's the point? ,

She's barely older than the group of boys—the pool-players gawking at her shyly. She could make some cash tonight. But she ignores them, comes to the bar. Orders herself a drink standing close so her shoulder brushes mine, her side warms me.

"I got it," I say, pulling out a fifty. This is not my normal behaviour. Musta hit my head when I met that tree. Gets me thinking of that Oldsmobile piece of crap, that blue-smoke-blowing gas pig whale I kept shined up so nice. A little bodywork and it'd be fine. True for so many things.

"Pauline," she says.

This gets me thinking about how I don't want to walk home tonight. I can afford a room upstairs, one of those died-in rooms, those rooms wallpapered in loneliness. Might as well try for someplace nicer. Pauline probably doesn't live upstairs, her face would have to be more sunken in, more beat down, for that.

"God damn Oldsmobile," I curse. Pauline is sympathetic. She is swinging thin hips in the air to the song, Roy Orbison now. In a different place I might ask her to dance, she wants me to, her brown eyes say so.

"Got any blow?" she wonders. She'll be snorting lines off my balls by the end of the night, I can tell.

"No," I lie. "Coupla joints though."

The joints are laced anyway. We step out the sheet-metal side door into the back parking lot. The boys are fish-mouthed. One elbows the other and they try not to giggle. They probably went to school with Pauline, they probably know her. I can't find my Zippo. There's a rusted pickup rocking back and forth under the heavy branches of a maple tree. We pretend not to notice.

She's got matches in her tight jeans. I light, she inhales, stretches her neck side to side, and drops her head back to study the pinpricks of light in the sky. She's got a nervous edge to her: a little high-strung, the way she jitters, the way she steps anxiously from foot to foot. This isn't the place to give it away for free. We both know that. But I'm not gonna bring up price. It's more fun this way, to see how steely she can be, to see what she might say.

wild birds

"*I didn't* do nothing," Jellybean said.

The school principal stood in the frame of his office door. "Come in, Jacqueline. This is Mrs. Freemont."

Mrs. Freemont wore a baggy animal print dress. Her jewelry was too big and her bangs were too straight. She looked like a social worker.

"Hello, Jacqueline, please call me Bernice," she said from her chair. Bernice had a clipboard. Jellybean didn't trust people with clipboards.

Mr. Mathews invited Jellybean into an empty chair. "Last week your class was given a writing assignment, correct?"

"I did that already. I handed it in."

Mr. Mathews sat at his desk. "Yes, we know. Listen, it's important that you understand you're not in any trouble here. We just want to talk to you."

Jelly sucked her lips into the space between her teeth and bit down. Mr. Mathews continued. "Would you please tell us the topic of the assignment?"

"We had to write a page on what we wanted to do when we growed up."

"Grew up."

"Yeah. Like I said, a whole page."

Jelly wore a denim miniskirt and an adult-sized sweatshirt with a picture of a diving eagle on the front. She pulled the hem of the sweatshirt down and covered her legs. Then she brought her knees up to her chin and rested her heels on the edge of the chair.

"Jacqueline, Bernice is here to discuss your paper with you."

The lady stretched a ringed hand over to the armrest on Jelly's chair.

"Now," she said in a voice that sounded slow and far away, "let me start by saying you wrote that paper very well."

Jellybean shrugged.

Bernice's voice was thick. Jelly wondered if Bernice was dumb. But then she decided dumb people didn't carry clipboards.

"Did anyone tell you to write this...ah...topic?"

Jelly shook her head and pulled the cuff of her sweatshirt sleeve down so it covered her left hand.

"No? Was it a dare? Did any of your classmates dare you to write this paper?"

Jelly covered her mouth with the cloth of the loose sleeve and began chewing on the cotton cuff. Who would dare her to do her homework?

Bernice sighed. "Well then, I guess I should start by asking you about your aunt. Why do you love your aunt?"

"'Cause she's my aunt."

"Yes. Of course. But what is it about your aunt that you admire so much?"

"Dunno." Jelly chewed harder at the sweatshirt cuff, ready to move to another question. Bernice and Mr. Mathews watched her, saying nothing. Finally Jelly decided she'd have to give them more. From behind the soggy sleeve, Jelly recited some of the lines from her paper.

"I like my Auntie Pauline because she wears beautiful clothes and lives in the city. Her clothes sparkle and have jewels and feathers sewed into them. Her shoes are high heels all the time and she never wears gumboots. She is the prettiest girl in the world. Sometimes she lets me wear her shoes."

Bernice smiled. "Go on."

Jellybean could remember every word she'd written about Auntie Pauline.

"When Auntie Pauline visits everyone is happy. Mom cries and says 'So good to see ya.' Auntie Pauline always has presents for me and my brothers and sisters. We order pizza because Auntie Pauline always has money."

When she finished, Jelly could hear Mr. Mathews breathing. Then her stomach made belly rumble thunder.

"Does your aunt ever talk to you about her job?" Bernice asked. Mr. Mathews pulled a drawer in his desk and lifted out a box of Toffees. Jellybean watched as he opened the lid. She never expected the school principal to have chocolates in his desk.

"Go ahead," he said softly. He put the box on the edge of the desk closest to Jelly. "Have as many as you want."

Bernice repeated her question.

"Um, yeah. We talk lots when she visits. We go and sit at the beach and talk about how when I'm old enough, I can live in her apartment downtown."

Bernice nodded. "Do you think your aunt's job is a good thing to do?"

Jelly slipped the wet shirt sleeve back between her lips, then spoke through it. "Auntie Pauline says lots of people don't like it but they're hippocreeps."

Bernice looked at Mr. Mathews.

"Do you mean 'hypocrites'?" he asked.

"Yeah. Like I said. Auntie Pauline says she could walk into any bank in the city and see familiar faces."

Mr. Mathews seemed to smirk. Jelly took another candy.

"Auntie Pauline says it's what most of the girls from the island end up doing when they go to the city anyway. And it's pretty safe, with the rudders and everything."

Mr. Mathews started choking. He made a fist to cover his mouth, coughed, and slapped his chest.

Bernice squirmed. "One of the things we're most concerned about, Jacqueline, is why you admire this...particular...occupation. Usually it's the sort of thing girls want to avoid."

Jelly had heard that before, but she didn't think Auntie Pauline would lie to her.

"My Auntie says 'A girl's got to do it anyway, so she might as well make a living.'"

"But what do *you* think about it?"

Jelly gnawed her sleeve. "I don't get the big deal," she said quietly. "I mean, everyone's supposed to like it and it's all people seem to talk about. So, well, it seems like a pretty good job."

Bernice re-crossed her legs. "What does your mother think about this?"

"She didn't read my paper."

"No, I mean, what does your mother think about your aunt?"

Jelly shrugged. The air in the office was getting hot. She dropped her legs off her chair and swung them.

"Have you ever talked about this issue with your mother?"

"I dunno. I guess. Sort of."

"And what did she have to say?" Bernice leaned close. Jelly didn't know how any of this could get her in trouble, but she recognized something hungry in the way Bernice smiled.

"I have to go to the little girl's room."

Mr. Mathews shrugged. "You're right," he said. "We've been

here a while. This might be a good time to stop."

"Jacqueline," Bernice said, sloth-tongue slow, "I am going to come back tomorrow, so we can talk again. Would that be alright with you?"

"Are you going to try to call my mom?"

"Do you want us to?"

"No." If they did, they'd know the phone was cut off again.

"Well then, for now, you and I will just talk some more. Okay?"

Jelly didn't want to talk to them but she knew she would. There was no other choice.

II

I liked bird watching. I had a field guide and a good pair of binoculars. When I rented my house it was mostly because of the eagle perch trees across the road. The brown A-frame was dark and had a mildew smell grown into the carpets but faced south to the eagle trees.

I was busy down at the quarry, new on the crew. I didn't get much chance to explore the woods around the house, and when spring came up with the crocuses and violets, I couldn't believe all the birds. Robins aren't so special, except in my yard, where they flit through the grass twenty at a time. The pileated woodpecker started knocking in my backyard and I could watch his red crown bobbing from where I sat with my morning coffee.

Little ping-pong chickadees, starlings, even the occasional hummingbird came by with its helicopter hovering. It was good I didn't write all the sightings out or count them, 'cause I don't know if I could count that high.

One morning I came home from the pit, pissed off at being relieved late. The sun was stretching over the tips of the cedar trees and the eagles were in their perch, backs to me, beaks to the ocean. I heard a warble.

It was a liquid, smooth chirp that rolled over four or five times. I dropped my steel lunchbox on the porch and turned to face the woods. I waited. Silence. I picked up my lunchbox. The warble came again. It was a fast, happy chirping that swung from a high to a low note in a soft wave. It came as a single, long song; not staccato like the woodpecker; not whistled like the eagle. I put my lunchbox down again and slipped into the trees.

My boots sank into soft moss as I kicked through the bracken and sword fern and ducked under low cedar arms. The melody was a swallow dive-bombing for mosquitoes. It was a swan gliding onto a flat pond. The composition reverberated through the trees, a lulling, swooning circular psalm. One trill carried over and up and around and down. Then nothing. I stopped in green shadow and waited until the bubbling cry began again.

I got closer. It got louder. I imagined what the bird would look like and at first I dreamed of silver wings with a grey breast shimmering blue in moonlight. Then I dreamed a canary yellow like the sun. But no, I had to be realistic. This would be a small brown bird dabbled in black—a flighty chameleon I'd overlooked.

As another symphonic line gurgled closed, I burst out of the salmonberry bushes as if I was leaping off a cliff into winter water.

The bird's song stopped and a tiny, black-haired girl screamed.

I put my hand out like a crossing guard. She stared. She was an elf, a little pygmy girl. She had a green plastic toy in her hand, which she clutched to her chest.

"Did you hear that bird?"

She stayed still, her eyes huge and her neck bent back so she could see the top of me.

"There was a call. A bird call. I've been following it."

I looked over her head, scanning for strange birds on the wires. I had come out of the bush into someone's dirt driveway. There was a small cottage with wood smoke puffing from a shiny metal stack in the roof. A tricycle was on its side in the dirt, and a kid's cardboard fort leaned against a prim wood pile hidden under the eaves of the house.

The little girl lifted the toy to her lips. It looked sort of like a pipe, with a molded plastic bowl and a short, green mouthpiece. Her cheeks puffed like a trumpet player's and the warble song rose from her hands.

"Well, I'll be . . ."

She played a short tune and then stretched her hand out to me. I took the whistle. The bowl was shaped like a fat bird with an open mouth. The belly was filled with water. I lifted it to my lips and puffed. Water spurted out of the plastic bird's mouth and the little girl giggled. On a second attempt I blew much softer. The same song I'd heard through the trees came out of the green whistle.

"Who are you?"

I looked up and a woman was standing at the door that had been shut a moment before.

"Name's Wayne." I gave the little girl her toy back and winked, which made her giggle again. I stepped closer to the door. "I live in the A-frame on the other side of the trees. I was following a bird call."

The woman wiped her hands on her jeans and came down one step from the door. "The whistle?"

"Yeah, well, I never heard anything like that before and I sort of like watching birds, you know."

The little girl had gone to the cardboard fort to watch us. The woman smiled. She had a crooked sort of grin. The muscles on the right side of her face didn't seem to work as well as on the left. This made her appealing.

"You could hear all the way from your place?"

"Yeah, well, I was outside."

I realized I was still in my work clothes. My checked shirt was missing one sleeve and I'd pulled the front pocket off a while back. My jeans were ripped and faded. I was powdered in rock dust that stuck to sweat and made my skin as rough as a dog fish. My hair was grey as if I was ninety. But the woman didn't seem to mind. She took another step toward me and stuck out her hand.

"I'm Moira."

"Wayne."

"You said that already."

I looked at my work boots and Moira glanced over at the girl in the box. "That's Jellybean."

"How ya been, Jellybean?"

She giggled and chortled her whistle.

"So you work at the quarry?"

"Since January."

Moira nodded. One of her sleeves had fallen and she rolled it up.

"How do you like the neighbourhood?"

"It's great. Great birds. Great trees. How about you?"

"Yeah. I've been here a while, though." She paused and scratched her head. Her hair was the same raven colour as the little girl's, but cut in a short, spiky way. "I've got coffee on."

"Thanks, but I shouldn't come in. I'm gritty."

"Right."

"But thanks, though."

Moira nodded.

"Maybe some other time?" I suggested.

"Maybe."

"Okay, well then." I looked at the bush I'd come through and then down the driveway to the road. The bush was quicker but the road was more dignified. I scuffed my boots down the driveway, waving once to the little girl who played me a plastic Sousa song to march me away.

The next day I was lying in bed when I heard gravel crunching in my driveway. I got up and hopped into some jeans. There was a knock. I pulled on a t-shirt. When I opened the door, Moira shoved a pie toward me.

"We made this for you," she said. I took the pie in both hands and she squeezed past me in the doorframe.

"Should have done it sooner, you know, to welcome you to the neighbourhood. But I forget stuff like that. It was Jelly's idea."

I put the pie on my counter and followed Moira into my living room.

"Is her name really Jellybean?"

"Nah. Jacqueline, but nobody calls her that."

"Where is she?"

"School."

"Oh. Why wasn't she in school yesterday?"

"It was the weekend." Moira glanced around.

"I'll put some coffee on," I said, going to the kitchen.

"Did you read all these books?" Moira called.

"Yep."

"That's a lot to read. I wouldn't have thought..." but then she stopped.

"It's okay. Most people think that, well, you know, because I don't say much, or because I'm big, they think maybe I'm slow or something."

"I don't read many books. Not since school. Not even then, really."

"I like to think while I'm working."

Moira dropped into a chair and I leaned on the wall between the kitchen and living room. "What do you think about?" she asked.

"You know, just words."

Moira scrunched her brow but there were only wrinkles on the left side. "I got five kids," she said. "The other four were at soccer when you came by."

"Boys or girls?"

"Two boys. Three girls. Total."

"That's a lot."

"No dad, though. I mean, no dad now. We're all alone. Just the six of us."

I nodded. "Six doesn't sound too alone." I went into the kitchen, poured hot water, and mixed the instant coffee.

"They're not all mine, though."

"Who aren't?"

"The kids."

"No?"

"The two boys belong to my sister in the city. She can't take care of them."

"So you do? That's nice."

"Yeah, well, I may not be the best mom but I'm better than some, you know?"

"Should I slice this pie?"

"Sure thing. I was going to make blueberry, but Jelly said not to. She said you were an apple pie kind of guy."

"Yeah, I like apple."

Moira had some loose shingles falling off the sides of her house. I had some red cedar blocks and experience as a shake splitter.

Moira needed seaweed for her garden and I had a pickup truck, a tide schedule and a strong back. Jeff and Joel needed to learn Cub Scout skills and I knew how to sharpen a hatchet and make a good fire. The older girls, Trisha and Danielle, they didn't think I was good for much until I took a stand on their allowance. Moira thought allowance should relate to what chores were accomplished in a week, while I believed it was a kid's weekly right to the price of popcorn and a movie. So they seemed to like me fine when I started handing out fivers on Friday nights.

And Jellybean, she liked me from day one. She liked birds. She liked to read. Although she wasn't old enough for most of my books, she liked being around them. She'd come over and run her hands along the spines on the shelves. She'd pick up a random book, flip it to any page, hold it to her nose, and inhale deeply. Then she'd tell me what she thought the book was about, based on the smell, or how I'd treated the pages. Sometimes I'd come back from work to a library totally reorganized by colour of the binding, or size of the lettering, or some other characteristic that was only rational to her.

I'd never dated a woman with kids before, never mind a handful of them. But after a while we cut a trail between the two houses. I figured out all five different ways the kids ate their eggs.

"Any chance I could get you to babysit tonight?" Moira asked. She leaned over my chest and dropped her pack of smokes onto the table. "Mrs. Stubbs cancelled."

"Sure." I lifted her cigarette, tapped the ashes into the ashtray, stole a drag, and handed it back.

"I wouldn't ask, except it's parent-teacher interviews, which I got to go to. And I got four teachers to see, so I can't really leave the kids alone all night. It wouldn't be any trouble. I'll have dinner ready and you just have to make 'em eat, turn off the TV and get 'em to bed."

"I spend plenty of time with the kids, Moira."

"Yeah, but usually I'm there, or you don't got all five. I mean, this is sort of a favour."

"I'll do you a favour." I rolled onto my side and kissed the tattoo on her shoulder. It was a blue peace symbol she got one night in Dawson City she couldn't remember. I spun a short, black curl from her forehead around my finger.

"You expecting any trouble?"

"With who, the kids or the teachers?"

I laughed. "Teachers."

"The boys aren't doing too well at their maths. The girls have been caught smoking behind school twice now, so I suppose I'll be getting a lecture about that. Anyway, I'll go out at five. You home from work at four tomorrow?"

"It's supposed to be four."

"Yeah, well, just so long as you're back by five."

I ran my finger from her forehead, down to her ear, across her tattoo. I got momentarily stalled while tracing her breast, then continued tracking downward, over her stomach. She giggled as I followed the curve of her belly. I stopped.

"Any chance you'd marry me?"

"I've been married before."

"Second time's a charm."

"We hardly know each other."

That surprised me. "We know each other well enough."

Moira laughed.

We'd finished debating whose turn it was to wash up after dinner when Jellybean presented a leather-bound copy of *Treasure Island*.

"Can you read it, Wayne?" she asked, handing it over like it wasn't mine to begin with.

"We want to watch *Diff'rent Strokes*," Trisha and Danielle whined.

The boys were in the kitchen with the dishes and didn't think I could hear them.

"Books are stupid," Jeff said.

"Like we don't get enough of them at school," agreed Joel.

I'd never read books out loud before. Jelly and I took up chairs in the living room corner. I made sure to take the words slow, curving and molding my lips as if I was exaggerating an instruction over pit blasting. My voice bellowed over the clanking dishes and the American commercials and by the time the black spot had been delivered, the other four were at my feet, mouths open.

Someone opened the front door. It was too early to be Moira.

"Let's get this party started!" a woman cried from the hall. I closed the book.

"Mom?" Both boys jumped up.

"Auntie Pauline?" The girls ran down the hallway. I stood and followed. She was a tiny, wiry thing. She looked all sinew, like she hadn't eaten ever. Her hair was big and frizzy. I didn't like the way she was dressed.

"Hi," I said.

"Who are you?"

"I'm Wayne."

"Well, kids," she said, dropping her bag and rubbing her hands over the heads of both boys. "I guess somebody better tell me who the hell Wayne is, and where I can find my damn sister."

The three of us were at my place, not wanting to keep the kids up after the struggle it took to get them to bed. Pauline and

Moira sat beside each other on my couch. Moira had square, strong shoulders; Pauline was slim and bird-like. Pauline's hair was long and dyed almost white so it looked dry and stiff as straw. Moira didn't bother with makeup. Pauline wore sequins.

"So he comes bursting out of the bushes, dressed in his work clothes, all ripped and covered in rock dust, looking for some ridiculous bird."

Pauline cackled and slapped her bare knee. "Musta scared pour Jellybean to hell and back."

"She thought it was funny," I said.

Pauline reached into her purse and took out a ball of tinfoil, some plastic straws, and a piece of cardboard with pins poking though it.

"I've got a good connection." She put down her cigarette and unwrapped the tinfoil.

Moira reached over and put her hand on Pauline's leg. "How long you staying, honey?"

"A week or so. I'm laying low."

"But you're going back?"

"Of course, why wouldn't I?"

"The boys miss you. They'd like a chance to spend some time with you is all."

"Right. The boys. But I've got things to keep up in the city."

"Yeah, I know."

"And the apartment. I mean, all my stuff's there."

"Just make sure you say goodbye this time, Okay? Last time was tough on all of us."

Pauline stayed a week. She had some drugs that were hard to get on the island and she had some good stories. But the girls started wearing makeup, and the boys lit the shed on fire.

When she left, she made a big production of it, as she should have. She gave the boys Swiss Army knives. She gave Trisha and Danielle a rainbow of oily makeup that came in a heart-shaped box. She gave Jellybean her sequined tubetop, which Jelly wore as a dress.

Pauline promised to call Moira every week, then she climbed into my truck.

"I appreciate the ride, Wayne."

I drove past the cemetery and turned toward the ferry.

"It's real nice of you."

"I drive the kids around all the time," I said.

"Yeah well, I appreciate the favour. I mean, maybe I can pay you back. Maybe I could do you a favour sometime."

I didn't respond until we got into town. "We're here." I turned off the engine. "You need bus change?"

"I've got my own money."

I didn't mean to insult her. "No, I just meant, you know, change for the bus. Sometimes it's hard to get change." I paused. "You are taking the bus, right?"

"I'll have no trouble getting a ride." She slammed the truck door.

III

"I'm sorry, boys, she said she'd be here." Moira sat on the edge of Jeff's bed and I leaned in the doorframe. Joel had insisted we wait until Pauline arrived before cutting the birthday cake. We opened presents and hung out until the last ferry was idling at the dock. Then Joel said we had to give her some time to get to the house. By eleven-thirty, Jelly was asleep and nobody wanted cake. But Moira lit the candles and we all sang. Earlier in the

evening, I'd given the boys copies of Jack London stories. I had something else in mind but Moira made me wait. She suspected Pauline wouldn't make it, since there hadn't been a phone call in over a month.

Moira kissed each boy on the forehead as she tucked them into their beds, then turned to me.

"Wayne, why don't you bring those boxes in?"

I went to the hall closet and came back with a stack of two light, square boxes. I put one on each bed.

"Go ahead."

They shredded the paper. They both opened their boxes and looked at the bicycle helmets inside.

"Happy birthday," I said.

Jeff took his helmet out of the squeaky Styrofoam casing, but Joel just let his sit in the box on his lap. "What do we need these for?" he asked.

"You can't ride bikes without them."

"We don't have bikes," he spat. "Remember?"

"Right. I forgot. Moira, the boys don't have bikes."

Moira smiled.

"I guess the only thing to do about that is get some bikes then, eh?"

"No way!" Jeff jumped from his bed, leapt halfway across the room, and knocked my breath out.

"Wow, cool," Joel said from his bed. He didn't move, or take the helmet out of the box, but he did smile a little.

Later that night I was lying awake listening to the different snores and sniffles filter through the house. Moira was asleep, sputtering the occasional syllable from some dream. I heard feet in the hall.

There was the clicking sound of the phone being lifted from the receiver. Moira hadn't been able to afford a phone until I moved in and since then it was the kid's favourite toy. We had a chart on the fridge that kept track of who could have phone time, how much, and when.

"I'd like a phone number please," a whispered voice said from the hall. "For Dick. Pauline Dick."

I got out of bed, picked my boxers up from the floor, put them on, and opened the bedroom door.

"Yeah, in the city." There was a pause and Joel stood in the glow of the hallway nightlight, his Star Wars pajamas looking too small for him. "Are you sure?"

He hung up the phone and I stepped into the hall. He looked up at me and exploded the way only kids can. Tears rained off his cheeks as he grimaced. His fists clenched and punched down the air.

I moved closer and leaned onto my knees. "Hey, buddy."

He wrapped his arms around my neck and cried into my shoulder. I stood and carried him into the living room so he wouldn't wake anyone.

"Your mother loves you, Joel," I said, passing my hand over his dark hair.

"No, she doesn't."

"Sure she does. She just has trouble sometimes."

"How come nobody else's mother is like her?"

I shrugged. "Nobody has parents like anyone else. But think of how lucky you are, you've got Pauline *and* you've got Moira."

"And you."

"Yeah, you've got me. See, you're pretty lucky."

"Wayne, do you know who my father is?"

"No. Sorry, man. I don't."

"How come? How come none of us know?"

"Maybe Pauline thinks it's better that way."

"Do you think she'll tell us if I asked?"

"When you're older you could ask. But you want to wait."

"Why?"

"Some things..." I shrugged. "It might be hard for Pauline to talk about it."

Trisha had stolen my truck again. Moira was passed out on the couch and no one had heard from Pauline in six months. I was in the kitchen making macaroni, debating whether I should call the cops, when I heard the truck pull into the driveway.

"It was an emergency," Trisha said before the front door was closed. She tossed the keys at me and I dropped my wooden spoon.

"Better be one hell of an emergency, Trisha."

She looked down the hall and saw Moira on the couch. Trisha rolled her eyes and kicked the shoes off her feet so they thundered against the wall.

"Marcy ran out of maxi pads and we had to get to the store before it closed, so there wasn't time to walk."

"That's bull." She was trying to embarrass me. "What about Marcy's parents?"

"Her dad's at work and her mom's in the city. You didn't want me to hitchhike, did you? I mean, she was practically bleeding to death."

"Couldn't she have balled up some t.p. and stuck it down her panties?"

Trisha crossed her arms and glared. "You're a pig."

"Well, you're a liar and a kid without a licence who's gonna end up doing time for grand theft auto."

"Your truck's not all that grand, Wayne."

Trisha covered her ears while I bashed pots. On the couch, Moira groaned and rolled over.

"No allowance this week. No television. No phone time. You

come home straight after school every day. You do your home-work at the kitchen table and I swear to God if I ever catch you in my truck again I'll have the cops after you."

Trisha gasped. "Who the hell made you the boss, Wayne? I don't remember inviting you to join this family. And before you were here, mom was on the wagon." She pounded her feet down the hall. "You're ruining this family, can't you see?" Trisha slammed the bedroom door.

I looked over at Jellybean who'd been sitting on the kitchen floor, reading. She shrugged. "Don't listen to her, Wayne. She's mellow dramatics."

"Am I the problem, Jellybean?"

She shook her head. "This is our normal."

I'd been doing a half-day at the quarry when the call came about Moira. She was at her friend Sheryl's house and drowned in so much home-brew she'd gone blind. Jelly went to her little buddy Colwyn's place after school and I had to take her to an optom-etrist appointment in the city. I wanted to rush to Sheryl's house, hold Moira. Then I decided not to. It would be better if I just took care of the kids, let Moira sort things out, and hope she'd come back to the way she'd been when I met her. The problem was Pauline, who hadn't called or appeared on the doorstep for almost eight months now. In Pauline's profession, if you don't hear from someone for a long time, you might not hear from them at all. So Moira had her pain and was pickling it well enough.

I picked Jellybean up at Colwyn's house and we headed for the four-twenty ferry. I didn't mention her mom.

On the ferry, after Jelly'd spent all the quarters I had in my pocket on some video game, she sat with me and we watched the smaller islands slip past.

"I don't want to wear glasses, Wayne."

"I know kiddo, but it'll be helpful in the end."

"The kids will make fun of me."

"Who will?"

"I don't know. But someone."

"How would you feel if I told you that you weren't allowed to read another book in your entire life?"

Jelly's mouth fell open. "Really? Why?"

"How would you feel?"

"I'd be mad. And sad."

"So there you go. You need glasses to help you read."

"I can read okay."

"You get headaches, I know you do."

"Yeah, but Mom has headaches all the time."

I sighed. "Jelly, it's not the same thing."

The optometrist was extraordinarily late.

"This is crap," I snapped at the receptionist. "The last ferry's in forty-five minutes."

The lady shrugged and flipped another page of her magazine.

"Do you understand we have a boat to catch?"

"Dr. Curll is just a little behind. I'm sure you understand. It's a Friday, everyone's staying late."

"Don't worry, Wayne," Jelly put her hand on my wrist and smiled. "If we miss the boat, we'll swim."

I tried to smile for her sake.

"Look, lady, I've got four kids at home to take care of, besides this one." I pointed to Jelly. "I don't think you understand that if we don't get out of here in the next half an hour, there's no way for us to get home tonight."

"I understand, sir." She flipped a page. "Most of our clients are from the island."

The pay phone smelled like piss. I had Sheryl's phone number inked onto my wrist. Jelly was in the truck, staring at herself in a little mirror. The glasses she'd picked were pink.

"We missed the last boat," I barked, when Sheryl answered. "Can you keep Moira?"

"Sure. Sure thing. Me and Moira are just having a good time." Sheryl's voice slipped and slurred.

"For God's sake, Sheryl, don't let her drink any more. We'll be back on the first ferry. I'll pick her up in the morning."

We drove around the city. Jelly stared up at the buildings. "Let's go see Auntie Pauline," she suggested quietly. "Mom's worried about her, and I bet she'd like my new glasses."

"That's a good idea, kiddo. But I don't know where to find her."

We spun around another block, silently watching the drab sidewalks and the slate silver windows.

"I know where to find her," Jelly whispered. "I never been there but she told me once."

I pulled the truck into a loading zone, left it on idle, and noticed how pale Jellybean looked against the bleak city background. "Tell me what you know."

"She lives in an apartment, number seven, in a building called Bush House. It's on the third floor. The building is red brick and she says it's real close to Woolworth's. She says she goes to a coffee shop called The Ovaltine for breakfast, and she goes to a fish shop called The Only for dinner and they are real close to where she lives. She says there's a statue in a little city park, and it's full of pigeons all the time, and she goes there at night to feed the birds. I bet that's where she is right now."

I studied the way her black hair parted and fell straight down past her shoulders. "Do you remember every word people say to you?"

Jelly shrugged. "Stuff I hear just sticks in my brain. Maybe I have a photographic memory?"

"Maybe."

"Let's go look for her, Wayne. It can't hurt to look, right?"

I shrugged.

I liked how Hastings Street had neon signs and how Gastown rumbled with train racket. We drove up and down Water and Hastings streets with our windows open. Jelly kept leaning out her window and pointing. The steam clock puffed as we rolled by. The Hotel Niagara's sign streaked neon water down to the street. On our third pass through I parked in front of the Save-On-Meats butcher.

"You ever been to Chinatown?"

Jelly shook her head.

"We'll go there for dinner. It's close to here."

"Yeah, we'll take Auntie Pauline."

"Just stay here." I locked the truck doors and walked the few steps to the crosswalk. But looking back at Jelly, I saw her making faces against the glass. I went back.

"Come on, kiddo. Hold onto my hand and don't stare at people."

We crossed the road to Pigeon Park. There was a small crowd, gritty rubbies and thin women in impractical clothes.

"What have we got here?" One tall, heavily made-up woman squeaked as we approached the park. She smoked a cigarette while leaning on the shoulder of a shorter woman with wild hair.

"Dirty birds," said the short one.

The crowd evaluated me first and then Jellybean. I was just another guy who'd come to the city and stepped out of his truck. But Jelly was a raven-haired elfling in pink glasses. She smiled gently and squeezed my hand. Some of the women looked longingly at her fresh face, while others hissed at me, and stepped away.

"I'm looking for someone," I stuttered. A few people turned back to their conversations or moved to the other side of the pointy monument and kicked up a cloud of fat pigeons.

"Dirty birds foul their own nests," warned the short woman.

"A date?" The tall woman asked. She didn't seem to blink. "We're all looking for someone."

"No. A particular girl. Her name's Pauline. She's young, twenty-four or so."

The woman dropped her cigarette. "She lives down here?"

"Yeah, she's got an apartment. In Bush House, I think it's called." This brought a sneer from the tall woman's face. A man sitting on a bench at my side spoke from behind his brown layers.

"Check the corner," he said. "Them Bush House girls are always up there."

"The corner?"

"Up on Main."

The tall woman squatted to Jellybean's level.

Jelly smiled. "I like your shoes."

The woman smiled so her lips looked like a red slash across her face.

"Well thanks honey." She glanced up at me and down my arm to where I held Jelly's hand. "You okay down here, hun?"

Jelly nodded. "We're looking for Auntie Pauline."

The woman stretched herself up again. "Check the corner, ask around," she said. "I don't know any Paulines, but you know how it is." She shrugged and pulled her jean jacket over her bare shoulders. "There are lots of names."

"Right, thanks." We moved away, but then I turned back. "Couldn't we check the apartment building?"

The woman shook her head, nodded her chin in Jelly's direction. "Lots of people come and go," she offered.

We crossed back to the truck and I drove up to the Main

cross street. "Stay here. I'm going to lock the doors."

"I want to come too. There's The Ovaltine, look at the sign. We're close."

"I'm just going to go over there and talk to some people. You'll be able to see me the whole time and I'll be able to see you."

"But that building's a library."

"I don't know if it is or not. Maybe it just used to be a library." The corner of the street offered a rounded staircase rising into a granite building with a cupola on top.

"I want to come." She pulled the lock open on the door and hopped out.

"Jelly, it might not be safe."

"Why wouldn't it be?"

I took her hand and we crossed the street to the library steps.

"Excuse me," I said to a man with a blue bandana on his head. He dropped his eyes and shuffled away.

"Pardon me," I approached a pair of tired women who were too gaunt and jittery to judge their age. They turned their backs. There was one woman, a sturdy-shouldered gal in army boots who leaned in a doorframe a few steps away. She'd been staring at us since we got out of the truck.

I gave Jelly's hand a light tug and we walked to the army-boot woman. She was obviously studying us, taking in every detail of Jelly, then me.

"Pardon me," I said as we got close enough to speak. "I'm wondering if you could help me."

"That depends," the woman said quickly. "What did you have in mind?"

"I'm looking for a young girl."

The army-boot girl's face contorted, and then her arm snapped as if she were a snake making a strike.

"Sounds like trouble to me," she spat, grabbing my free arm and twisting it behind my back. Suddenly she was behind me and I was being pushed into the doorframe with my face imprinted against red brick.

"Let's go have a little talk," the army-boot girl whispered.

I had to let go of Jelly's hand as the woman forced my left arm back.

"No, you don't understand," I cried. "This is a misunderstanding."

Jelly screamed, "You let go of Wayne." Then she kicked the woman's shin. A pair of uniformed police officers came running across the street.

"Well, then," the undercover cop said. "Let's go work it out."

IV

Lit up the way it was, in crepe paper and Christmas lights, the Mason Hall looked like a magic fairy world. Mom gave me, Trish, Danielle and the twins, each a wrapped present to put on the gift table at the back of the hall. Everyone from the creek was there: Jake Snowflake, the Ruth sisters, Colwyn and his mom. Islanders always had a dance for Father's Day, but I'd never been to one before.

Colwyn was sitting under a long table, spinning a rainbow-coloured top over the grooves in the wood floor. I crawled under the orange tablecloth and sat cross-legged beside him.

"Whatcha doing?"

He shrugged. Someone from the band was onstage, practicing scales on a long horn. When Colwyn's top fell on its side, I scooped it.

"Can I try?"

He shrugged again. My spin got caught in the pit where a nail had been pounded in.

"What's wrong with you?"

Colwyn nodded his chin toward another table, on the other side of the dance floor, where a family I didn't know was sitting.

"There goes my old dad," Colwyn said. His chest sagged.

"Where's your new dad?"

"Probably with his old family. Where's Wayne?"

"I don't know. I haven't seen him in a while, you know, since I come back from the city. Think he'll come tonight?"

"He might. But what if he's already got a new family."

"Wayne wouldn't do that."

"Sure he would. That's what dads do."

I lifted the corner of the tablecloth and scanned the room. Kids were running around chasing balloons. The moms were at tables, dads standing around with thumbs hooked in their belt loops.

"Wayne couldn't have a new family by now. He's not even allowed to have my family."

"Yeah, that's too bad. What did he do?"

"I dunno. We were in town looking for my aunt and then an under-the-covers policewoman took me away. I just got back last week."

"My mom says your aunt isn't coming back."

"Shut up. That's not very nice." I scrunched my eyes. "Why you gotta be so mean?"

"It's not me," Colwyn said. "Look, there's my dad from the dad before."

"You wanna get some punch?" There was a table in the kitchen spread out with all kinds of good food. I'd seen it when I put my present down.

"We're not allowed punch."

"Some juice then?"

Colwyn shook his head.

"What did you come here for if you're just gonna sit under the table? Come on, let's go to the kitchen."

A pair of thick, hairy legs came toward the table. The legs bent as the faceless man sat down, knobby knee bone sticking into Colwyn's face.

"Who's that?"

"I don't recognize him." Colwyn snorted. "Probably some new dad."

"You're such a pestamist." I grabbed his elbow. "Come on, let's go get juiced."

It was the spread of food I noticed first: the falafel balls and pita bread, veggie burgers, paella, smoked salmon, fry bread, and all kinds of squares and cookies. It was only after I'd made a close inspection of the buffet, that I noticed him, standing against a corner of the kitchen, smiling.

"Waaynnne!" I ran across the room and leapt into his arms. "Hey, you gotta haircut." I stroked the top of his head where his long, blonde hair had been shaved off.

"Good to see ya, kiddo." His voice didn't sound too excited but he was smiling huge. He tossed me over his shoulder and walked over to Colwyn.

"How ya doing, buddy?"

"Alright."

"Hey, Wayne, come on in," I said, waving my arms toward the hall. "Everyone's here, they all want to see you."

Wayne swung me down to the floor, then squatted so we were eye to eye.

"I can't stay long, Jelly. I just wanted to drop in, you know and say hi."

"Hi."

"Hi. How's your mom doing?"

"She's fine. Better. She got that money you sent."

"That's good. How about the boys? How they doing?"

"They burned the shed down to the ground."

"Good." Wayne laughed. "What about the girls?"

"No more truck left to steal. They been hanging around the house, you know, painting their nails."

"And how about my Jellybean? How's she?"

I wanted to smile but for some reason I started crying. "Not so good, Wayne. Not so good." I wiped my nose on my sleeve. "We miss you. When are you coming back?"

"That's why I'm here, kiddo, I wanted to explain. I won't be coming back."

"Don't say that." I stomped my foot. Colwyn moved to the kitchen door and leaned against the frame, his back to us. "I'm sorry. I didn't mean to get you in trouble. I'm sorry. Please come back."

Wayne put one hand under my chin so I had to look at him.

"I know this is hard, honey. No one wanted things to be like this. You got to believe I wouldn't ever choose to leave you guys. But it isn't my choice, you know?"

"But why?"

"I can't explain it, kiddo. There's been some confusion and once things get this mixed up, there's not much a guy like me can do to straighten it out. Best for all of us if I just sort of disappear."

I gasped. "But you can't leave the island!"

"No, I'm gonna try not to. But I can't be your step-dad anymore."

"That's so stupid!"

"Yep. It sure is." Wayne brushed tears off my cheek with his thumb. "Will you send a message to the gang for me? Tell Moira I'm sorry. Tell the boys to stop setting fires. Tell the girls to be good. And you...you just keep being Jelly. You're okay, kiddo. You'll be just fine."

Wayne straightened up and walked toward Colwyn. "You two have fun," he said, and rubbed his hand through Colwyn's dark hair. Then he smiled and walked out the back door of the hall kitchen.

V

Five years without hearing from Pauline, and the Smokecrest Indian Band decided to have a burning. Jellybean was twelve, the boys thirteen, and the girls had moved to the city after finishing high school. I hadn't seen any of them in a long time, which is hard to do in such a small place. But after Moira stopped drinking and got the kids back from foster care, I didn't want to sneak around with her. It wasn't worth the risk, having the kids taken away. The social workers still checked in on those kids regularly.

I didn't want to cause trouble. But I knew Pauline and I knew her kids and her sister. I'd sat with her and given her a ride in my truck, so there was no way I was going to miss the burning.

Clarence was on the porch of the Dry Goods having a cigarette when I pulled in.

"Hey there, Clarence."

"Hey there, Wayne."

"I heard about the burning."

"Yeah. Bear Clan's real sad about all that. But I guess it's time, eh?"

"I'd like to be there. I mean, I knew Pauline. Not real well, but I knew her."

"You were looking for her in the city that time, weren't you, Wayne?"

"Yeah."

"So you knew her."

"But I'm still not supposed to be around, and Moira would be upset. She's working so hard for them and all."

"She misses you, you know. She told Hannah and Hannah told me and now I'm telling you. Go on back. No one's going to cause you two trouble up here."

"Those social workers come up sometimes and check things out. That's what happened before. I went to say goodbye to the kids and someone saw and then they got chucked in that foster care. Moira was drinking and they thought I was some sort of weirdo, taking Jelly to that part of town."

"Well you should come to the burning, anyways."

"I don't know how I'll be able to do that."

"You're as good as family, anyways. I'll talk to Hannah. She's Bear. She'll figure something out."

The four clans stood on the pebbled beach with the new totem poles behind them. The tide was the lowest of the year and the rocks were green with seaweed, the air salty and thick. Clarence and some of the older folks were decked out head to toe. Red and black blankets outlined in glowing buttons draped off their shoulders and down to the ground. Some of the hats were woven and looked sort of like cedar bark lampshades. Other hats were braided bands with shells and masks punctuating the middle. There were fringed vests, beaded moccasins, bright yellow and black capes and wide, moon-faced necklaces.

Moira wasn't dressed traditional, though. She stood with the elders of Bear Clan like a shadow against a field of wild flowers. All five kids and Moira herself were completely in black.

Noah Smoker came down the beach to the beating of drums, and the group gathered around the small fire in a circle.

"Welcome," Noah said when he'd moved to the inside of the circle. He passed the sage smudge around and when it came back to him, he added it to the fire and spoke again. "We will bless this burning with eagle downs."

Auntie Mona passed him a small square box with a handle on the top that was a carved eagle. The lid could barely contain the white tufts and when Noah pulled it off, a cloud of feathery snowflakes swirled around his head. He flung the downs over us to spin in the air and kiss everybody standing at the fire.

Mona stepped in front of the fire ring and all the women sang.

"We are here for our daughter, sister, mother, auntie, cousin Pauline. Pauline who left Smokecrest. Pauline who would come back to her island if she could."

Food spread out on cedar slabs was carried by one member of each clan and placed in the flame.

Moira put a photo of Pauline in the fire, then she cut a lock of her black hair and dropped it to burn.

Joel burned a map of the island, a map of the city, and a copy of his birth certificate.

Jeff burned a pair of moccasins, a pack of cigarettes, and her favourite Ramones record.

Trisha poured a bottle of gin onto the circle of hot rocks around the flame, which sizzled and steamed juniper-scented mist to our faces.

Danielle placed some dried flowers, ten dollars, and a tabloid newspaper to burn.

Jellybean burned the tube top.

Noah and Mona and all the Clan leaders said blessings, and then it was time to dance. I was getting hot in my costume, under the heavy bearskin and thick wooden mask. I danced the way Clarence and Hannah had taught me. I danced with the Eagle, Cougar, and Raven. The drums pounded and the voices wailed high. As I pawed at the ground and the air and growled my best bear, I saw Jellybean smile, then Moira, then the boys. Trisha and Danielle elbowed each other. They knew who I was. They knew I was there for them, and we were all there for Pauline.

the smoker

Ralphie Louch had woken up in worse places.

His vision blurred as he rolled his cheek away from the ground and took in the canopy of dry-skinned arbutus.

From the curve of the road next to him, or maybe the sound of the waves below him on the beach, he sensed his location. He was on the island. Smokecrest had found him in the night.

This happened more than Ralphie wanted to admit. Clean and sober, he did everything he could to get away from the island; forget about it; live a life denying all the familiarities the place bred into a boy. Man. Whatever.

Ralphie did his best to avoid the island. Then, every so often, on a particularly good drunk or nice week-long cruise on one drug or another, he'd find himself stranded.

He'd come to in a backyard or truck box or a boat stored on a lawn. He'd be able to sense his location from the smell of the grass, the hush of the waves, or the fact that houses in the city didn't have many backyard boats.

Ralphie rubbed the scarred side of his chin, wondering what he'd been thinking, what could have been going on in his autopilot brain that would drag his sorry ass home. Again.

"Hey-ya. Ralphie." The voice sounded annoyed, and far away. "Shake off those leaves and come on over."

Ralphie rolled to his knees and blinked. The shapes of houses began to form their square ridges in his sights. He had fallen asleep in the Landing, the little cluster of small wooden houses built one on top of the other, on the granite hillside. He was just out of town; a fair walk from the dock where the ferry pulled in. The calling voice was vaguely familiar. Ralphie stood and squinted. She was waving an arm from her balcony. The moss and wild chives still had a coat of dew.

"You're up early, Cat," Ralphie grumbled when he got to her yard. He avoided the house and walked to the deck on the side, where Cat was leaning against a banister of curved wood worn smooth.

"Nice of you to visit, Ralphie," she said without a smirk or smile. "Coffee?"

"Oh yeah." He stomped up the stairs to the deck, and made a brief accounting of his belongings. He had on two boots, shirt, jacket, pants, watch, hat on his head. So it hadn't been a wild night.

Cat went to the kitchen, filled a mug, returned with it. Ralphie lowered himself to the top stair step and planted his elbows against the insides of his knees.

"You're pregnant, you know," he said, taking the offered mug and pointing at her belly.

"And here I thought it was just a pimple." Cat negotiated the deck chair in an uneasy squatting motion until she was eventually sitting.

"You probably shouldn't be drinking coffee," he meant to be funny.

"You probably shouldn't be doing half the stuff you're doing," Cat said quickly, then added, "Mine's decaf."

Ralphie looked out at the flat water spread between them and the next island across the gap. The air wore a wood smoke scent, fir burning hot with a little red cedar mixed in. He couldn't help identifying the aromas in his head, a reflex from his Boy Scout days, when Hammersmith drilled those sorts of facts into him.

Cat was younger, yet to Ralphie she seemed decades older, in her little house with her big belly. His clothes felt damp and his teeth ached at the contrast between the hot coffee and cool air.

"Where's Thomas?" he asked, thinking Thomas would be out working, playing the rugged mountain man, ripping down trees with his bare hands.

"Asleep."

"Not out, hard at work, putting us all to shame?"

"Hard work shouldn't put you to shame, Ralphie."

"That's not what I meant and you know it. I'm just surprised your superman actually sleeps."

"Yeah, well," Cat paused to sigh. "My superman has a nice bed to sleep in." She didn't want to be hard on Ralphie. Yet she had to try. "You're too old to be waking up on the side of the road, you know."

He could feel a lecture coming on. That was the price of a cup of coffee on the island, always had been.

"Haven't you ever wondered if you've missed out on anything?" Ralphie struck the offense. "I mean, really Cat, I remember you. I remember you ten years ago, going to punk shows, wearing army boots. Didn't you ever want to just take off and never come back?"

"Like you?"

"I've been around, you know? I've been to Montreal and New York and London. I've hopped railcars, slept in haylofts, survived more bar fights than maybe I deserved to. Point is, I've been living it. Really taking it all in."

"You make it sound glamorous."

"That's not what I mean."

"But we both know there's another side to the story. You've been in more jail cells than I'll ever see. You went to Montreal to do the Angels a favour, and you rode railcars to get there because you had no other choices. Heaven only knows what you did for enough money to go to New York and London. But you presumably snorted or drank or shot all your cash away, because it was your dad who paid for the ticket home and everyone on the island knows it."

"That's exactly why I hate this place."

"You don't hate this place."

"I do."

"Well, maybe you do hate it. But you're quick to come back every time you forget."

"Yeah, and quickly condemned every time I do."

"I'm not condemning you, Ralphie. I wanted to get away. We all did. But..." she didn't know if she could say it.

"What?" he was trying not to sound angry, but it wasn't working. "Spit it out."

"Maybe you're the reason we all stayed."

"Yeah, you're right. I'm the grand master of the universe who has control over every kid on the island a few years younger than me. Everyone does what I say. You really hit the nail on the head with that one, honey"

"You're older than me. I admired you, growing up. You're tall with a tricky smile. We loved our local bad boy off at art school. Coming home to visit in your black leather jacket and studded bracelets, you seemed cool, for a while."

Ralphie absently fingered a raised ridge across his chin as she continued.

"We started hearing about bar fights. Drug deals. That time you almost OD'd. Your dad started a fund for rehab costs. But after you beat up that girl—"

"She was no girl."

"—doesn't matter, Ralphie. It doesn't sound good. Your dad visited you in a boardinghouse that was little more than a jail cell. You had no bedding, no niceties. You go out each day and live life on the pavement, wake up on the concrete, surround yourself with brick and steel. Those stories made me reconsider leaving."

"You're not me, Cat."

"But Ralphie, that's my point. You're not you, either. So where did you go?"

"I'm me." He was quick to defend. "And you? You did what? You stayed here, stayed safe. Got a bun in the oven and a little house with a view. How exciting. Big deal. What am I, dead already?"

"You really think you're going to get to where I am from where you are?" Cat didn't mean to sound so dubious. It was a collective wish that he would.

"Could if I wanted to." His leg bobbed up and down in agitation. Cat knew he'd get up and leave soon, and it might be years before she saw him again.

"I know you could," she softened. "You could do anything."

His flinch was visible. "Why have you always been nice to me, Cat? You're too nice."

"'Round here, a cup of coffee in the morning is no big deal."

"No, but I know you. You'd give me your car if I needed it. Give me cash if I was broke. You'd dress me, feed me, talk my ear off and tell me I was better than the life I'm in. You've always been that way, sort of looking down on me ever since you were a little squirt."

"I think you misinterpreted my interest."

"You always make me feel like some kind of pity project."

"Because I care?"

"You've got no right caring about me."

"This is the island, Ralphie," Cat said, "I can't be anything but me."

"Same goes for me."

Cat nodded, having to accept Ralphie, tattooed, scarred, a hard product of a place that raised her soft.

Thomas came to the door wearing grey Stanfield leggings and nothing else. He rubbed his hands across his bare chest, his habit to wake himself. "Who you talking to?" he asked Cat through the gap in the sliding glass. Then he took in the form on the stairs as Ralphie turned to face him.

"Well, Goddamn," Thomas offered. He threw open the door and walked to Ralphie, quickly grabbing him in a hug before Ralphie stood. "Good to see you, man. Cat, why didn't you wake me up? You been here all night?"

Ralphie shook his head.

"Come on in, we've got breakfast. Cat—" She was already struggling to get out of the deep deck chair. Ralphie offered her an arm and Cat felt how thin his strength was as she pulled her awkward bulk against him.

"On its way," she said and went into the kitchen. As Cat broke eggs and sliced bread, she heard them outside laughing and slapping each other's backs. The men had a much different kind of conversation.

"Want to make a few bucks, Ralphie? Come out on the water with me for the day." Thomas was always willing to give a friend work.

Ralphie squinted for a moment, scratched the skin of his shoulder where an abstract shape from a large, black tattoo bloomed beneath the rolled-up cuff of his shirt. This was the sort of trap he always ran into on the island.

"Well, not today, anyway," Ralphie said, forgetting to add a thanks. "I should see Pop, you know, drop in on him before someone mentions that they saw me."

Cat and Thomas nodded. It was a reasonable excuse. Ralphie helped clear dishes from the table, then went back out to the deck and lit a cigarette.

Lights were on in the other houses around the hillside. Smoke coughed up from the cluster of chimneys. It wasn't a harder, meaner life that he looked for off-island. It was anonymity. The freedom to not be talked about. Only problem was he'd never found it. If Cat had somehow heard about Montreal, the Angels, there were no secrets.

On the city streets no one expected anything from him. But a small town has expectations. Every time he woke up on the island, Ralphie felt the burden of every wrong he'd every committed, every derogatory opinion rightly thrown his way. Ralphie didn't think he was born bad, and he didn't think the island made him bad, but he knew the island wouldn't let him forget anything bad he'd ever done. So it hemmed him in, kept him reprobate, made him what he was.

"Gonna walk," he called into the house, not wanting to be cornered by Cat again. Thomas was struggling into his hip-waders and mackinaw. It wasn't raining, but the clouds were low and looked concrete, promising rain.

Thomas raised one hand in goodbye. "Good to see ya, buddy," he said.

Cat moved to the door and waved.

"Thanks for the grub," Ralphie said from the bottom of the stairs, facing away. He shifted bony shoulders under his leather jacket, and then started up the hill, past the spot on the side of the road where he'd woken, and walked in to town.

Orren Louch was sitting under the covered verandah of the Dry Goods store. He'd run the place for almost forty years. He'd done no other job in his life, except for the farm work and simple labour any teenager does, before being placed behind the counter of what would become the centre of the island's business community.

Orren figured he was lucky to keep the same, decent job, to have an income he could count on, and a nice pair of rent-free rooms in the upstairs of the building. As far as Orren could tell, he'd been lucky in life. Except for losing Ingrid to that cattleman from the prairie and raising a good-for-nothing son.

It was hard to say if Ingrid's abandonment caused Ralphie's bad streak. Ralphie wasn't twelve when Ingrid ran off but he was already setting fires, messing around with girls in the bushes, stealing cigarettes from the store cabinet, sneaking out at night.

After Ingrid took off, stock started going missing from the store. Orren never told people how much it hurt him when he had to tighten up security at the Dry Goods. Crime had come to the island, he told folks. But he never told them he'd raised his own troubles.

Orren liked his Ralphie fine. Smart kid, just a little misguided. When Ralphie came home from school with broken ribs and black eyes, Orren paid little mind. He figured he'd let Ralphie work things out of his system. Sometimes Orren hoped someone would knock some sense into him.

Orren let Ralphie mind the store on his own, figuring if he felt some ownership over the place, maybe cigarettes and magazines wouldn't keep disappearing. But stories started filtering back about how rude Ralphie could be behind the counter, insulting customers, skimming cash from the sales, closing up early to go down to the pub.

Orren knew it was his job to discipline his son, but he could never bring himself to do it. Ralphie would just stare at him, blink a few times, look hurt or shamed, nod to acknowledge Orren's anger, and then go out and do whatever he'd been doing, just the same.

Islanders seemed relieved when Ralphie took off for the city, and for a while, Orren shared the feeling. His son turned up on his doorstep six months after moving, tattooed, beaten, shaking badly. Orren put him in the shower and fed him soup, washed his clothes, watched Ralphie shave with an unsteady hand.

It was the start of a pattern. Months of silence and absence broken by a knock on the door in the middle of the night. Ralphie appearing wet on the doorstep, bearing nothing but stories and a chip on his shoulder that seemed to grow like a tumor. They'd drink a few beers if it was evening, coffee if it was afternoon, and Orren would listen to the same promises.

"I'm gonna get it together," Ralphie always said. "Something's got to change, Pop."

Orren always nodded and always wished it were so. And then Ralphie would disappear and Orren would hate himself for hoping.

So that morning, when Orren saw Ralphie's figure coming up the empty Main Street, he had enough warning.

Orren poured the rest of his coffee onto the rhododendron bush that grew against the store's stoop. He tugged at his belt as if securing himself against something, and then he went into the store, flipped the sign from "Open" to "Closed", locked the door, and sat behind the counter.

"I can see ya in there, Pop," Ralphie said, his forehead pressed against the glass of the front door. "What's up?"

"Actions speak louder than words," Orren yelled from his place at the counter.

"Let me in."

"No."

Ralphie took a moment to look left and right, survey the street, see if anyone was watching.

"I could just break the door, what's the point?"

"Point is, you're not welcome."

"Aw, come on, Pop. That's not very nice."

"Each time you come back here, you smoke my cigarettes, drink my beer, tell me things are going to change. Each time I believe you. Then you take off and there's a bit of cash missing from the register. Someone mentions they saw you on the ferry and that's the only way I know you've left. Folks shake their heads. I've had it. You can't come in. This isn't your home."

Ralphie wanted to argue but it was no fun with a locked door between them and no beer. He just shrugged. "Alright then," Ralphie said to the door. He walked down the steps and back down the street.

Orren went to the window to watch his son go.

"Hello?" a voice called from inside the house. Ralphie knocked on the front door again, ignoring the ring in the mouth of the brass lion that hung on the frame.

Cat opened the door and Ralphie threw his arms up to cover his face as if she were going to beat him.

"Come on in," Cat said, suppressing a smile. "Your dad not home?"

"Wouldn't let me in." Ralphie grabbed an armful of wood from the stacked pile beside the door, and walked into the house with purpose.

"About time."

"I thought I'd go work with Thomas."

"He's already out." She gestured to the water, where a small grey boat disappeared into the horizon.

Ralphie shrugged. "So you wanna hump, then?"

Cat exploded with laughter, caught off guard. "Good luck!" She ran her hands over her immense belly. "Come on," she moved into the kitchen. "You can help me bake."

Ralphie put his load of wood down next to the stove in the living room and brushed splinters off the front of his shirt. "Can I put on some tunes?" He began flipping through options. "This is a good stereo."

Cat waited for Ralphie to choose music and join her. She was glad for a moment to think. She'd already yelled at him. What else was there to do?

"I'm making a pie to take over to Mr. Dick. He's been sick for a couple of weeks and this might cheer him up."

"I hate sick people," Ralphie offered. When Cat said nothing, he moved beside her and gently nudged her away from the counter. "Besides, you're making it wrong." He took the spatula out of her hand and tossed it into the sink. "Your crust will be like cardboard." He opened drawers until he found the utensils, took a fork, and began pressing the tines against the clumps of shortening in the flour.

Cat leaned against the fridge and watched as Ralphie mixed the dough, formed a ball, floured the counter and began rolling out the pie crust.

"Where'd you learn to bake?"

"I did cooking for a few years, trained under a couple of really smart guys. French style, you know. Lots of sauces and stuff. And pastries."

"Where?"

"Banff. A couple of hotels in the prairies. You know, here and there. What do you have for filling?"

Cat pointed to a saucepan on the back of the gas range. She'd stewed and strained a pumpkin from the garden the day before.

"Nice," Ralphie said. He dipped a finger in to taste the orange mush. "Got any nutmeg?"

Cat searched her spice drawer.

"What about ginger? A little grated ginger would really pep this up." Ralphie turned the element on and began stirring. Cat filled her mug with the decaffeinated coffee still in the coffee pot and got comfortable at her kitchen table.

When Ralphie went into the fridge for cream, he also pulled out the pork loin that was defrosting. "I could do a stuffing if you wanted, roast this baby. There's rosemary out in your garden, right? I saw it when I came in."

Before Cat could answer or rise, Ralphie dashed out the door to pick fresh rosemary. When he returned, the oil of the herb filled the kitchen and the baby in Cat's belly made a slow revolution, as if moved by the perfume.

They spent the rest of the day in the kitchen, Ralphie's mouth moving as fast as his hands. He chopped, grated, sautéed, diced. Pies cooled on the counter and Ralphie hand-whipped cream to garnish. The windows steamed up so they couldn't see the water, and Ralphie's cigarette smoke darkened the air. Cat finally let him smoke inside when the rain broke.

"Will you come over to Mr. Dick's with me? I mean, this is your pie, not mine."

Ralphie remembered the time he broke into Clarence's shed and stole tools to sell for a fix in the city. "Think I'll just have a little nap on the couch, if you don't mind. You go ahead."

He waited until Cat pulled out of the driveway before kicking his shoes off and sitting down. The old Ralphie would have gone straight to the medicine cabinet and rifled through for anything interesting. Instead, he flicked on the TV.

Cat drove slowly around the winding road that hugged the

curves of granite. The water was calm and flat, the ocean surface fuzzy with the dimpling rain. She'd never spent a lot of time with Ralphie. She was surprised at what a good companion he'd made.

When she pulled up into the driveway, the chimney blew out a thin trail of smoke. Cat wrestled herself from behind the steering wheel, then carried an armload of wood inside. The house was hot and rich with the spice of the pies and the roast.

Ralphie's bold snores came from the living room. She glanced in to see pillows tossed to the fir floor. Ralphie, curled into a slightly fetal position, hid his face in the couch corner between the back and armrest. Cat put the split cedar down beside the wood stove as quietly as she could. She brushed splinters from her sweater as she backed into the kitchen.

Ralphie had done all the food prep for the day. The kitchen was clean. She could sit quietly beside him and watch TV, but that was creepy. So what to do? Cat's eyes scanned over the familiar surfaces and paused on Ralphie's cigarettes on the windowsill.

A smoke would be nice. Cat inhaled deeply at the thought. She'd never been much of a smoker. Thomas didn't approve. He ripped smokes out of friends' mouths and called them cancer sticks and coffin nails.

But sometimes when she drank, sometimes when she just needed...something, a smoke did the trick.

Cat told herself not to, as she picked up the red package and shook one cylinder out. She shouldn't, she was pregnant. But one smoke, so late in a pregnancy, one smoke couldn't make a difference, she was sure.

The deck at the back of the house, with the Adirondack chairs and expansive view of the harbour was the nicest place to sit.

Cat avoided it for two reasons. First, she didn't deserve it, if she was about to do something so bad. And second, neighbours like Emily and Mike Harvey, lived only a few feet away on either side of the deck. Cat didn't want anyone noticing her smoking this single contraband.

She wanted the secret as much as the smoke itself.

She sat outside her front door with her back nestled into the woodpile, where the angles were perfect to hide her from neighbours on all sides. Cat pulled her sweater over her knees and flicked the lighter a few times before bringing the flame to her face.

The first deep drag made her dizzy. She relaxed her back into the stacked wood and shook her shoulders loose of tension. She felt foolish, childish, her knees pulled up to her chin, hiding against the wood shed with a stolen cigarette. But it was fun.

Perhaps this was the last time she would feel so young, she considered.

Motherhood made her nervous. She suspected she'd have to give up on youth entirely.

Initially, such a forced hand for the sake of adulthood seemed appealing. She was a married woman with child, and therefore must be an adult. But as the months of gestation slowly wore along, Cat realized the ability to breed didn't make her any more adult, any more together, than she'd been months before.

She still longed for things like night swimming and roller coasters, a trip to Europe, a convertible. Being pregnant hadn't changed that longing. It was reconciling her reality with her desires that became the hardest part of the pregnancy. Expectations come double-edged.

She thought about Ralphie in her kitchen, chopping ginger, his nails gripping the beige skin, the large knife skimming against the guard of his bent knuckles. Maybe there was no such thing as "together." Maybe having life together was a myth, and one just lived it as it came, waking up in a ditch one morning, or waking up pregnant and married, depending.

The phone rang inside. It could be Thomas on his radio-phone, or else she'd let it ring. Cat rubbed her smouldering cigarette against the damp step and tossed it to the grass at the side of the house. She got the phone on the third ring, but it had already disturbed Ralphie. As Cat greeted the caller, Clarence thanking her again for the pie and wanting to get Thomas's help with something, she studied Ralphie's features as he woke.

First his face was blank and open, soft, not yet awake. Then there was fear, as he scanned his surroundings and had to run through a mental list of where he might possibly be. A flash of recognition, then his shoulders fell from his tight defensive pose. He rubbed his eyes and cheeks in the palms of his wide hands, and Cat couldn't help but wonder what his face felt like, his cheeks hot and flushed from sleep, that hard ridge of a scar burning a cold line across his palm.

"Got any beer?" he asked after a few minutes of sitting on the couch, watching the water. Cat pulled a bottle out of the fridge and brought it in to him. She watched his fingers fidget as he went to toss the bottle cap across the room, caught himself, and dropped it into the breast pocket of his shirt.

"You care what we watch?" He had the remote in his square fingers and flicked rapidly through channels. "Nothing on."

"Ralphie, what are you doing here?" Cat asked in her softest voice, so that he wouldn't see it as a challenge, but more a question of interest, or bewilderment.

He shrugged. "Dunno yet. I mean, here I am. Life's just funny that way. You end up somewhere, play it out, go somewhere else. Sure beats nine to five in a dark suit, you know?"

He settled on the music video channel and turned up the

volume. She sat beside him on the couch. With a sigh, Ralphie stretched his arm along the back of the couch just as Cat leaned back. She softened into the crook of his shoulder, both of them staring straight ahead at the flashing video scenes.

"You hear that?" Ralphie asked.

"What?" They were silent.

"Nothing, I guess." Ralphie's arm slipped off the sofa back and fell across Cat's shoulders.

He smelled good. Salty and fresh, with a hint of tobacco and ginger. Cat looked up to study the map carved into the left side of his face. Ralphie looked down at her, his eyes flecked with gold.

"Sure you don't hear something?" He wondered, not looking away.

"Just music." Cat looked at Ralphie's lips, then up to his eyes, his short, black hair with just a few traitorous grey strands.

His lips were soft and warm when he kissed her. It was a gentle, slow kiss, and felt natural to Cat, maybe inevitable. He pulled away and then came back, his hand in her hair, and Cat put her fingers lightly to his chin and traced the path of the scar.

"I hear something," Ralphie said, breaking away.

Cat figured he was just worried, imagining things. But she didn't mind when he stood up, alert, looking around. She had gotten what she wanted and she didn't need anything more. She was too dizzy to hear much beyond her own thudding heart and loud thoughts, already reprimanding her for what had barely happened. Ralphie turned the TV off and both of them heard it.

"Sounds like something's crackling, back here." Ralphie went down the hall to the front door. Cat was right behind him, the noise sounding familiar. Ralphie opened the door to a wall of flame. Cat screamed and he slammed it shut. "The house is on fire!"

"There's a..." Cat felt nauseous and leaned against the fake wood panelling in the hall. "...fire extinguisher in the kitchen."

Ralphie pushed past Cat, but then turned, grabbed her hand, and pulled her with him. "You need to get out of here."

She pointed to the red enamel canister stowed behind the pantry door. Ralphie grabbed it and dashed out the sliding glass doors and around the side of the house. Cat felt sick, knowing exactly what had happened, the only reason there was for the side of the house taking flame. She followed Ralphie, but by the time she got to him at the front of the house, the fire extinguisher was empty.

"Didn't make any difference," he said, tossing the canister into the flaming woodpile. The entire front wall was ablaze, an edge of the carport was just catching, and the front door, which Ralphie had opened only minutes before, was now white-hot with flame.

"What about a garden hose?" Cat hoped this could still be reduced to an anecdote: The time Mommy almost burned the house down, but didn't.

"Call the fire department, Cat. I'll back your car out of the carport. You should have a few minutes. You can grab a few important things if you hurry."

The time Mommy snuck a smoke and destroyed the entire house.

Cat dialled the number to the Harvey's gas station and rammed her message over the friendly greeting.

"Mike, it's Cat. The house is on fire. Get Wally fast."

"Your house or my house, Cat?"

"Mine right now, but yours could go too if you don't get here fast."

Cat hung up and then froze, staring at her sofa, her bookshelves, Thomas's music collection, family photos on the walls.

What was important?

She grabbed a wooden curio box her grandmother had given her. Then she picked up the throw rug Auntie Mona had helped her weave. She remembered the new clothes and toys in the baby's room, put her load of stuff down on the kitchen table, and started down the hall.

"Cat, stop!" Ralphie bellowed. She hoped he would slap her. She needed it. But instead he took her hand. "You need your purse. Put on some shoes. Grab a sweater."

Cat followed his orders, only vaguely aware that the flames at the end of the hall were hot and visible. The ceiling was beginning to darken with smoke.

"Does Thomas have his wallet with him?"

Cat nodded.

"Good, let's get out of here." Ralphie ushered Cat out of the glass doors, hesitated for a moment, grabbed his pack of smokes off the windowsill, his open bottle of beer from the kitchen table, and joined her outside.

"It's my fault, Ralphie."

"It's some freak accident."

"I stole a smoke while you were sleeping. I hid beside the woodpile."

Ralphie stopped, blinked a few times, studied her. "You didn't put it out?"

"I thought I did. I mean—ouch." The baby kicked as if it were a bird trying to break through its egg shell. Cat held both palms to her belly. "What else could it be?"

Ralphie shrugged and took a swig of beer. Then he opened his pack of smokes, put one in his mouth, and offered one to Cat.

"You have to be joking."

"Hypocrite," he said with a smile. Cat was incapable of being light-hearted at the moment. The heat from the fire was beginning to be unbearable where they stood, and as far as she could tell, she was standing outside with the Devil while her whole life went up in flames.

Cat opened her mouth and gulped a lungful of air, readying herself to berate Ralphie's inopportune sense of humour. But he cut her off before she got out any words.

"Let's just say I did it. When Wally and the boys get here and manage to put this thing out, I'll tell 'em I was smoking beside the woodpile, must have dropped an ash into some tinder. You have insurance, right?"

She nodded. "What would be the point?"

"Way I figure it, you're gonna be hard enough on yourself over this, for one thing. You might as well not have the entire island knowing what happened. Besides, doesn't this seem more like something I'd do than something you'd do? The island will suck it up. Give them all something good to vilify me over until my next visit."

Cat and Ralphie didn't risk the path running up the side of the house to get to the road. Instead they cut through Emily and Mike's yard and walked up to the steep road where they could hear the fire truck a few turns away. Ralphie had parked Cat's car on the other side of the road, leaving room for the fire truck to pull up to the house.

The clanging bell of the Wally One could be heard over the cracks and sighs of the flames. Wally and the Smokecrest Volunteer Fire Department had raised money for the red flat-deck truck with oil drums and a pump on the back and a bell spot-welded in a frame to the top of the cab. The volunteers met weekly down at the Inn and practiced mental drills and actual drinking. The truck was stored in front of Wally's house, just down the road from the Harvey's gas station. Since someone was always at Harvey's, and both Mike and his father were members of the SVFD, folks were instructed to call the gas station if they had a fire.

When the rare calls came in, the men sitting on the stools at the gas station counter put out their smokes, finished their coffees, and half-jogged in a group down to the fire truck. Someone would turn the key, waiting patiently in the ignition, while another knocked on Wally's door.

If Wally was home, he drove. If he wasn't home, one of the Harveys usually took the wheel. The rest of the men jammed into the truck cab and flanked the outsides, standing on the running boards and holding tight to the handles attached to the roof.

The men on the running boards spilled from the sides as the truck slowed, and Mike Harvey came running up to Cat.

"Anyone inside?"

"I'm right here, Mike."

"It's my job to check." Mike didn't acknowledge Ralphie. "Thomas at work?"

Cat nodded. "He should be on his way home soon. He'll be able to see the smoke from the water."

Mike turned and yelled an all-clear to the other men, waiting with fire hoses unfurled from the truck.

"It was my fault," Ralphie said quickly. Cat whapped him across his chest. Ralphie drained his beer and tossed the bottle into the bushes across the street. "I was smoking a cigarette out back. I must have dropped ash in the woodpile."

"Shut up. Mike, I was the one smoking. I was the one who lit the woodpile on fire. It was me, not Ralphie."

"Yous don't smoke, Cat," Mike said with his back to her, distracted by the action. "Yous got insurance, right?"

"Yes, I have insurance. And yes, I do smoke, I mean, I smoked today. Smell me."

Mike turned to face her, looked her up and down and frowned.

"It could have been either of us," Ralphie said. "We were both smoking, under the eaves to keep out of the rain."

"Yeah, well, I don't really care, now do I?" Mike said. "Alls I care is we put it out."

Thomas didn't waste any time asking questions. He lumbered up the hillside in his waders, looking like a swamp thing. Moving both arms simultaneously, he pulled Cat to his side and struck Ralphie across the jaw.

Ralphie shook it off as Cat pushed herself away.

"You idiot!" she started.

"I leave you alone for a couple of hours," Thomas tore into Ralphie as Mike Harvey stepped in to block another blow.

"Yous need to calm down, eh Thomas?" Mike tried.

"I saw smoke from the water. Do you know how many terrible thoughts I can come up with on that boat ride home?"

Cat crossed her arms defiantly. "Well, I'm okay, if you're interested in asking."

"I can see that you're okay or I darn well would have asked. But the house..." Thomas's voice squeaked like a little boy's. There wasn't going to be much house left by the time the fire was over.

"Well," Ralphie sighed, looking at his watch. "Guess I best be going."

Mike put his arms up to Thomas's chest to block another lunge. "Sorry about the fire, man," Ralphie said. "Hope things turn out."

The baby kicked Cat hard enough that she yelled. Then her water broke. The panicked look on her face was dramatic enough to get Thomas' attention.

"What's wrong?"

"You mean other than the house burning down?"

"Yeah, other than that." Thomas tried to read her.

"It's time to have the baby, I think," Cat said. "I'm sorry."

Thomas was already ushering her in the direction of the car. He screamed orders at Mike Harvey and the other firemen as he loaded Cat up, revved the engine, and tore off up the road.

"Who started the fire?" he asked bluntly, once on the road.

Cat spoke between exaggerated breaths. "I did. But Ralphie wants to say it was him."

"It'd be easier that way." Thomas spun through a series of hairpin turns. Cat made faces at each one. "Why'd you start a fire?"

"I didn't do it on purpose. It was an accident."

"Of course, I mean—"

Cat felt she'd been honest enough, for the moment. She focused on her breathing and ignored her husband until he parked and came around to help her out.

Auntie Mona and a group of aunties stood at the entrance of their silver long house. "We've been expecting you," Auntie Mona welcomed with a toothless chuckle. She pointed at the sky.

Cat's elbows were supported by aunties.

"Ooh, you smell like smoke," Mona crooned, as she ushered Cat inside the circular entrance. Cat paused, looked back at Thomas and waved.

"No uncles," she called to him. He blew her a kiss. Cat disappeared into Auntie Mona's care.

Thomas was left outside, alone, watching the smoke rise up from the other side of the island.

too long gone

Hannah opened her door and tossed compost scraps toward the place where the front lawn broke into pebbled seashore. She whispered a word in her mother's language, then went into the kitchen, lit a cigarette, turned down the heat on the stove and dropped a ham steak into the sizzling pan.

The phone rang but Hannah felt busy. She had no curiosity about the call. They could try again. Outside, seagulls quickly cleaned up the compost. The ocean was flat and the afternoon mist became a deeper grey with every minute. Out on the water, she thought she saw an unlikely interruption in the bland horizon, so she flipped off the burner.

Hannah had a thick fur wrap that Clarence had made for a birthday gift years ago, before he'd gotten the job down-island, when he'd had time in the winter to trap. Each pelt was a perfect match with the next: a collection of mahogany short hairs that suited her brown eyes and skin. Clarence had trapped, tanned and sewed the pelts into a long, thick garment. She knew Clarence must have caught them high up the mountain because of the length and thickness of the fur.

On cold nights, Hannah wore the wrap around her shoulders when she went to bed naked. In the bedroom, the fur became a sign between them that it was a night to keep warm.

When she went to the city they called her weasel wrap a mink stole and treated her with more respect when she wore it.

In her step-softened moccasins, her house jeans, t-shirt and the long, weightless fur pulled around her like a small blanket, Hannah left her kitchen to investigate the water.

"'Bout time," Gilda Dick called from the stoop next door.

"I thought I saw somethin'," Hannah answered softly, squinting at the water.

The two women stared out at the ocean.

"I seen it a couple a times, a minute ago," Gilda said. "Must be four of 'em out there, at least."

On the water, a sudden geyser of mist exploded toward the clouds, then gently disappeared.

The exhalation startled Hannah. "Been a long time," she said.

Gilda nodded and wrapped her arms around her barrel chest. "Not even. I never seen 'em here. I only heard the old stories, you know, 'bout how they used to visit."

"Ayy-yeah," Hannah said softly. "I remember. They used to visit us every season."

As the words left Hannah's lips, a brilliant black dorsal fin, rigid and bold, cut through the water. The killer whale's back rolled and his fin dove. He waved his tail at the women on their doorsteps. Then another whale breached halfway out of the water, rolled sideways in the air and sent up a tidal wave of wake as it crashed back down. A smaller orca poked out its nose and lifted itself from the water to flash a white belly, then tossed its head back and disappeared. The pod made horse-like gasps as they cleared their blowholes and took in gulps of air. A mother whale and her offspring breathed together. Hannah knew they would always match each other's rhythms, exhaling and inhaling in unison for the rest of their lives.

She shivered and glanced down the row of houses. All of the

front doors faced the water. "Where are our cousins?"

Gilda shrugged. It was late afternoon. Usually the reserve was busy with cars and dogs, kids on bikes, the occasional tourist snapping pictures of the poles.

But not just then. Just then, Hannah and Gilda were in a blessed moment: the children hypnotized by afternoon cartoons, other women managing their households, men in their trucks coming home tired.

An orca slapped a side fin against the water the way seals do at night. The sudden clap broke like applause at the end of a play.

"Best be gettin' back," Hannah whispered.

"Yeah, Martin'll be hungry too," Gilda said. She glanced over. "I've always liked that fur you're wearin'. Can't catch fur like that around here anymore."

Back inside her kitchen, Hannah again placed the fry pan on the burner. As the cast-iron warmed, she quietly sang one of the old songs. It was a song for a friend who'd come back from a too-long-gone journey.

When she looked out the window again, at the end of her song, the water was flat and the whales had moved on. Hannah turned back to cooking. She buried both hands into the bannock mixture that filled her old glass batter bowl. Back when her mother had used it, the bowl had been a crisp crimson red. But the bowl had been chipped and scraped and the red had left flake by flake. Now it was only Hannah's memory that kept the milk glass cherry.

wax boats

The single salmon trying to fight upstream doesn't have an easy time of it. It's too late for spawning and the autumn is too dry—there's barely any water in the creek bed. The salmon fights, but is doing a better job of bludgeoning itself against the dry boulders than launching itself home. The skin on its sides peels off, puffy and bleeding. Its fins are a sickly grey. This fish is closer to death than to dying.

I've seen lots of things on this island that could hurt a man's heart if he were inclined to feel it, or turn a man more into stone than anything else—as if hard work and a rural life had the same slow effect that Medusa's eyes might. It was no tragedy, that salmon.

One bloated fish trying to do the world right by beating itself up a dry creek bed is no great loss. But I remember when the stream gurgled with so much force the air was thick with water, and damp moss grew on the rocks, the trees, the telephone wires. I remember seasons when the creek was a writhing mess of fish, so many fat salmon returning home to die together, it made me proud to stand on the small bridge and consider the lives they'd lived, the dangers survived.

But this year, too late, just this one. It seemed like it had led a healthy life, that big fish. The golden sun with its late autumn heat blinded me and I closed my eyes, felt my sagging eyelids warm, and wondered if the salmon understood that it was alone.

An island is a miracle, a simple thing. To be cut off is somehow to be entirely whole, and to know your boundaries is to truly know yourself. Some folks can't stand the pressure of an island; for them it's a green jail cell, an ocean-bound cage. But an island is like a body—finite yet infinitely new with each exploration. Like the way one becomes accustomed to the little bumps on a lover's elbow but never actually expects them. That's like knowing the island, familiar but never rote.

People here *believe* in boats and that makes them more real than they are to mainlanders. There is something sacred about a boat, the gentle brilliance of it, and the risk that comes with pushing onto water. A boat is always an attempt. Setting off on the ocean is like testing the ice with the weight of your feet—there's no knowing, not really, if you're meant to be there, if nature will allow you to pass on through.

I've owned a lot of boats. My first was a 12-foot skiff that pulled faster under oars than with its rough little two-stroke outboard clapped to the stern. I'd take that one to the city for weekends on the town, in a felt fedora and gentleman's gloves. I'd go to the Commodore or maybe buy a book. Play some pool. If I didn't drink too much, I'd find my way back to the shore and sleep under the bench seat with the bail bucket as a pillow. There were nights when I tried to pilot home on black water, few lights in the world, just the seals barking to each other and the creatures of my imagination lurking below. I've been nudged awake on beaches miles from home by strange girls in pigtails poking me with a tentative toe to confirm my apparent death. I've woken up with my boat nowhere in sight. Once, pirated off without me, twice left to drift, untied. One sank to the muck at the side of the dock all of a sudden, as if she just couldn't stay afloat a second longer. I've had a few old wooden hulls slowly slip under over time, but only that one that fell like a shooting star, one second an admirable vessel, the next a joke at the bar.

My favourite, though, is none of these runabout play toys. Nor the steel whale of a ferry boat, or the rock barges that load up at the quarry. I admire the old steamships that are now tricked up for the summer tourists and refuse to remember the hard, bitter, working families they used to shuttle from mill town to mill town. I have no fondness for those beak-nosed speed contraptions with their goliath outboards and nauseating grumbles. None of those boats ever meant much to me.

No, the ship of my heart is barely seafaring. It's a little wax boat, less than a foot long in size, weighing less than a pound, glowingly translucent in its soft, gentle form. But it bobs along well enough, on a calm day. It's got a "v" tip at each end so it's always sailing the right way. There's no way to direct it, no rudder, no motor; it is meant to be set adrift. There's a square compartment for cargo in the middle and nothing else. It floats.

I was sitting on a log that was lousy with worm holes, teredo eaten right through, a swiss cheese log, so hollowed out I could hear the wind blowing through it. I was sitting on the beach at the mouth of the same creek that salmon is struggling up today, and I was alone. A bicycle appeared at the corner of the road and came closer. It was one of those bikes with a long seat and streamers on the handlebars.

I pushed my tongue against my gums where my front teeth used to be, and adjusted the Pendleton ball cap on my head. I watched the bike get closer and tapped my cane against my thigh.

The kid riding the bike was one of those chinks. I guess you'd call him Asian today. He had straight black hair cut into some sort of bowl shape around his face. His eyes looked barely open, fringed in dark eyelashes. He was dressed the way kids dress— jeans, a t-shirt, sneakers. But he was wearing a cardboard box tied to his back with rope, as if he'd rigged up a packsack for himself out of what he could find in a basement.

He stopped the bike where the beach and the road and my log all intersected. The bike's kickstand wouldn't hold in the sand so he carefully laid the frame on the ground and then removed the rope straps from his shoulders.

"So, do you speak English?"

The kid squinted at me for a moment and I thought maybe he didn't understand. But then he said "Yeah" with a touch of insolence.

"I didn't know," I grumbled. I wanted to know what was in the box. It was large, but obviously not heavy. "Where ye from?"

"Here," the kid said with a shrug. He looked out at the water and considered the conditions.

"Bonnie day," I tried, also looking out.

"It will do," the kid said. There was a formality to his speech, a straight spine of a voice. He seemed like the kind of kid to take his lunch to school in a briefcase.

"I'm Old Man Bridgeworks." I like my prefix. I can't say when I got it exactly, but it's mine now.

"Colwyn," the kid said. I'd never heard that name before. Didn't sound too Asian.

"I never heard that name. Is it Chinese?"

The kid didn't look at me, just shook his head.

It's hard to tell the ages of young folks. This one wasn't too young because he had a bike and had rigged up the rope for the box. But he wasn't too old either, or he'd be driving a car, maybe find something a little less odd to carry around, like an old rucksack or something.

"I made three," the kid said. "But I won't need them all. I'm glad you're here." He bent down and started to unleash the rope from the cardboard. It was old floating rope that had been salvaged from a lost prawn trap or a found dinghy. I couldn't tell you what this Colwyn kid was talking about, but they were nice words to hear. It had been a long time since someone said something nice to me, and it gave me a good feeling. I wanted to give this kid something.

"I sit here," I explained, "because there's a kelp bed out there." I pointed to an imaginary line on the water where the pebble beach floor fringed into a garden of kelp and then fell to ocean depths beyond that. "You know that kelp bed?"

The kid looked up from stubborn knots. "Yeah, when the tide's low, the swimming here sucks."

I rolled my tongue against my cheek and nodded. No one likes swimming in kelp, it's like moving through wet rubber. Slimy and cold. It grabs your skin, sea onions rope at your legs, and there's nothing to see in the water but waving blackness.

"Whales eat there," I said.

Colwyn looked at me. "Killer whales?"

"No, them other ones."

"Porpoises?"

"No. The ones that eat kelp."

"Oh," said the kid.

"In spring, when they're passing through, they come to this beach. Water's high enough, they eat themselves a salad at that kelp bed."

I couldn't help but chuckle, remembering the sight. "They wave their tails around in the air as they're eating 'cause it's not deep enough for them. Their tails flap around, just out there, right off this beach. And they slap the water, flap against each other. All of them just hang around waving their tails for an hour or so, getting their feed. Then they go off and that's it. Won't see 'em again for another year."

Colwyn clearly liked the story because he stopped untying his knots.

"How many?"

"Once there were six."

Colwyn nodded and looked out to where he imagined the whales might be.

I tried to imagine what was inside the box. "What have you got in the box, lad?"

Colwyn scraped his fingers against the knots. They were not nautical; they were a mess.

"I could teach you to tie some proper knots." The rope he used was not one long piece, but a collection of smaller pieces joined together in an amateur style. "Didn't you do Boy Scouts?"

"No." Colwyn handed me two small pieces.

There was something wrong with that. All boys on the island do Boy Scouts.

"Improved blood knot," I said. "It's for joining fishing line, but it'll do here." I spun my wrists slowly, so the kid could see. The two pieces of rope turned and bent until they were one. "You try." I undid my work and passed the pieces over. Colwyn sat on the gravel beside the log and his bike and the odd box and looped the rope. It took him a few tries.

"Pull on that all you want; it won't come loose," I said. "You could bet your life on that knot."

Colwyn opened his cardboard box and pulled out a little wax boat. It glowed in his hands and he cradled it with reverence. "I made this," he said, passing it to me.

The wax seemed warm, as if the vessel was alive. "What for?"

Colwyn shrugged and reached into the box for two more boats just like the first.

"Make a wish," the kid said. He walked to the edge and set it on the water. The boat bobbed and rocked, rolled over the meek waves, then it nestled itself into shore. Colwyn picked it out of the water and came back to the box, shaking his head. He dried the bottom of the boat with the hem of his shirt and the thigh of his jeans. "You didn't make a wish," he said, and placed the boat back inside the box.

My cane fell from my hand. "I'm not the kind of man for wishing."

"Too bad," Colwyn said. "That's what the boats are for. I made them. They're Wish Boats. You put your wish inside them and push them off. If they go, your wish is in someone else's hands. If they come back, it's the wrong wish."

"Bah," I said. But I considered the glowing pearly white translucency of the wax. The boat seemed to know something. There was something smart in the soft shape.

"Well, what do you want me to wish for then?" I was annoyed. I was just sitting there, looking around, listening to the wind in the teredo holes. I wasn't prepared to get worked up with wishing. I'd wished for things as a younger man and did or didn't get them.

"Let's wish for whales," Colwyn said. He took the second boat to the water and set it down. It struggled and danced with the quiet waves, but began to move away. Not quickly. It left shore subtly, the way light creeps into the sky to make morning.

"When does it work?" I asked, still seeing the boat a short swim offshore.

"Whenever." Colwyn shrugged again. He was a weird kid. He closed his box and began to tie it up in his frantic scrabbled knots.

"There's this one," I reminded him.

"That's for you to keep. For your own wish."

"What about that one?" I asked, pointing to the box. Colwyn spoke as if all this should be evident and my questions were boring him.

"I have to take this one home and think about it," he said simply.

He put the box on his back and lifted his bike from the ground.

"Thanks for the knots, Mister."

"Thanks for the boat, lad."

He rode off on his bike in the opposite direction from which he'd come. The whales showed up three days later, but I never saw the kid again.

An old man like me doesn't need to wish. Got a fortune. Got a cabin. Got one grandson who comes by now and again to complain about all his family in the city, chop some wood, hack back the brambles, weed-eat the weeds. Got a town full of busybodies and a son minding the quarry. But there was something missing, I'll admit it. Not just my teeth or a pink feeling in the lung that used to come from a good, deep breath. There was something unfortunate about my life. Something solemn like a lone kid on a bike. A finality, like that beaten-up old salmon.

That boat Colwyn gave me sat on my mantle and bothered me with an entire year's worth of passing glances. Wishes were for suckers, and yet the whales had come. I didn't want to think about the boat, which meant of course that it preoccupied my thoughts from the moment I woke up until the night wrapped around me. I spent whole days considering the boat's construction, its purpose, and if I should try and put it to use. The enterprise seemed entirely foolish and yet not using it was also an insult, as if in not using it I confirmed its power and displayed my fear.

Finally I decided that a strong man could make a wish and not be fearful of the wishing. But I couldn't think of what I would ask for, I had no one to talk over such options with; even the fat dying salmon in the stream couldn't fish eye an answer when I asked it. I could wish for the kid to come back, but somehow that seemed pointless, and sad.

Everything seemed sad. My old Pendleton hat. My tiny cabin. My sore gums. If I wished for the kid to come back I could ask him what to wish for, but then I wouldn't have the boat. It was baffling, frustrating. It threw me. I grew angry at the kid for giving me the pretty gift, disturbing my peace. And then I moved through the anger to a deeper sadness, the feeling of being totally alone. At least at night I dreamed of a woman I loved, gone too long now. But even in dreams, for the longest time, she wouldn't offer me guidance for a wish.

Finally, as September was fading in golden leaf glory, I sat up in bed at five in the morning, woken from a dream where Harriet tugged on the thick hair I'd lost a lifetime ago. I put on my woollen long johns and stumbled through the dewy trail to the water, fast and full of purpose, my old cane flying. It was not a moment of despair or infinite sadness. No, it was a moment of decision, something clear and new after a lifetime of constant abrasion. I was a worn-down old man. I was tired. I was ready to go.

I shifted the honey-toned vessel from hand to hand, the wax so soft and oily against my swollen fingers I thought it might melt. When I got to the water I put the boat in and whispered, "Let me go. I do not wish to stay." I pushed it out with a great conviction, wishing for death, that moment, that day. The waves considered the wish, the boat rocked but didn't find a current to move on.

The little wax boat came back to me. Wrong wish. I turned

to walk home, make breakfast, feel the hours, suck at my gums, rattle my cane. I'd try again the next day, the day after that. I had my mind made up, was settled on it. That was the way things got done. Same wish, different day. I'd take the wish boat down to the water until it didn't come back to me, or I didn't come back to it.

acknowledgements

This collection of stories started as a poem submitted to Patrick Lane's writing workshop at the University of Victoria. Pat slapped my ass and told me "you'll be a great fiction writer, someday."

Jack Hodgins was the most thoughtful, careful, hard-working teacher I've had. He led by example, and gave me the courage to believe in BC as a place. He taught me arc, and mechanics, and gave a reading list to swoon over. My hours with Jack were the finest education I could have asked for, and I will forever be thankful for his belief in me.

Andreas Schroeder guided me line by line to write these stories. He is the kindest, most generous teacher I've known. He says "No masters drop from heaven." I am grateful for his apprenticeship. I will strive beyond this collection to prove his efforts worthy.

Nadine Pedersen, friend, editor, and writer, has been a great gift to me, and improved my life greatly. Thank you, dear goddess Nadine.

Patricia Wolfe was first to edit these stories and her eagle eye deserves high praise. She made me publishable and continues to have faith in me. She's sure I don't own a dictionary and yet she still works with me. Her friendship has been my very good fortune.

I'm deeply grateful for the skill and understanding of editor Meg Taylor. Thanks for catching my errors and coaxing out good solutions. I look forward to working together again.

Thanks to Jana Curll for her friendship and cover design.

Caitlin Press Publisher, Vici Johnstone, is a modern-day pioneer woman. She is brave, bold, and truly busy! Knowing Vici has been an enormous blessing. Thanks for having me at Caitlin, Vici.

Thanks to the inspirational Hammond family, the finest clan of writers/heroes/artists I've known.

Thanks to Catherine McManus, Cathy Kenny, and Garth David. Your support has been above and beyond.

Thanks to my beloved husband, Lane Eli Bingley, for "doing everything."

Thanks to the Canada Council for the Arts for generously funding my work.

I can't list how many more extraordinary people have helped me to become a writer. You know who you are. I am deeply grateful for your support, friendship, and encouragement.

Thanks to the characters of the Sunshine Coast. I am deeply grateful to live in such a wild, wonderful place. Come and visit us anytime, but please don't move here...The "island" is full.

Please feel free to contact me: www.sarahemilyroberts.ca.

Sarah Roberts is a graduate of the University of Victoria's writing program; her short stories have been published by literary journals in Canada, New Zealand, England, and the United States. She has worked as a writer with the Aboriginal Affairs department of BC Ministry of Forests, freelanced for newspapers and magazines, and has published as a ghostwriter. Sarah aims for her writing to reflect an Emily Carr painting—to explore the lush, spooky, dark forest of the BC Coast and surrounding waters, as well as encounter the unique rural characters found there. Her personal ethic is "Small Town," and she believes that the local is universal. Sarah lives in the town of Gibsons on the Sunshine Coast in BC, with her husband, Eli, a bird, and two tiny dogs. This is her first book of short stories. She is at work on her first novel.